PRAISE FOR

The Mooncatcher's Rescue

"Warm-hearted... A wonderful new
middle-grade voice championing those
who see things a little differently."

Sarah Baker
author of *Through the Mirror Door*

"A rip-roaring, soul-stirring adventure,
The Mooncatcher's Rescue simply brims
with magic. Utterly enchanting!"

Katharine Orton
author of *Nevertell*

The Mooncatcher's Rescue

KAREN LAMB

Illustrated by Lia Visiriu

WALKER BOOKS

First published 2022 by Walker Books Ltd
87 Vauxhall Walk, London SE11 5HJ

2 4 6 8 10 9 7 5 3 1

Text © 2022 Karen Lamb
Illustrations © 2022 Lia Visirin

The right of Karen Lamb to be identified as author
of this work has been asserted in accordance with
the Copyright, Designs and Patents Act 1988

This book has been typeset in Attaboy, Berkeley Oldstyle,
Marissa Moss, Neato Serif Rough and Sabon

Printed and bound by CPI Group (UK) Ltd, Croydon CR0 4YY

British Library Cataloguing in Publication Data:
a catalogue record for this book is
available from the British Library

ISBN 978-1-4063-8524-3

www.walker.co.uk

For Alexian, Melissa, Keyla and Evie.
Mooncatchers, all.

K.L.

For Marc

L.V.

Prologue

The ghost floating beside the pond looked up at the moon by Pointer's Peak and let out a moaning, groaning wail.

Sometimes, all it takes for a big dream to happen is something small.

(This wasn't the ghost's exact wail, but this is what the stars heard.)

Not all stories start
with a ghost calling to
the moon, a little village
with a pond so deep
they named it Bigdeepby
and a small boy called River
who loved to catch the moon there.
But this one does.

Chapter 1

An almost full moon hung over the street as River ran. He stuck to the shadows and cut through glints of light on cobblestones across the square. At the edge of the village, where the bulrushes began, he stopped to catch his breath.

A sleepy spring mist circled the clock tower as it struck the hour. His green eyes reflected the orange glow of cottages as he pushed back a flop of dark hair from his face. Behind the hush of reeds, frogs hiccupped, grasshoppers creaked, and a breeze came up from nowhere, parting the rushes, just a little.

River smiled. He was here.

Bigdeepby Pond gleamed before him like a new promise, as it did every night. There were the usual night sounds – the rustle of ducks settling in their nests, the soft click of rushes as water voles weaved through them, and far away, on Pointer's Peak, an owl hooted. River called back and the owl stopped mid-cry as if he'd fallen out of his tree. River wondered if he'd said something stupid in Owlish. Like owls are just tree chickens or something.

Shrugging, River kneeled beside the water, took off his backpack and opened it. He pulled out his fishing rod and laid it beside his net on the grass. As he reached for his bait box, a tangle of green and white fell out, stopping a snail in its tracks.

"Happy Spring Equinox," said River as he put on the leaf and snowdrop head-wreath. Everyone had made one at school. It had been the only good part of the day. He could smell the flowers, the scent stronger now they were dying.

A flash of blue and orange hovered before him: a dragonfly breathing tiny flimmers of fire.

"Hello," said River, calmly. It circled his head then darted off, skimming the water before disappearing above the reeds.

River sighed and laid the wreath gently on the surface of the pond. It drifted away as he looked for bait in his box. Shuffling through the compartments, his fingers came across three pennies. "For luck," he told a passing frog and threw them, one by one, into the floating wreath. Ripples grew as the greenery bubbled and sank.

Then came the sounds...

Cluy-uy-yung!

Cluy-uy-yung!

Cluy-uy-yung!

The pond wasn't called the Big Deep for nothing. The coins had struck something far below on the pond bed. River scratched his head and wondered if there was a cymbal or bell down there. He half-hoped for a submarine, and smiled, imagining a rusty periscope popping up.

He waited a long time, but nothing came

13

out of the water, not even flakes of rust. Whatever it was must be stuck in the mud, River thought, looking down at the pond. The moon was partly in shadow but appeared full in the pond's reflection. It had a blue glow about it tonight. River knew there would be plenty of fish with the moon so bright. And plenty of mooncatching.

After baiting his hook, River cast his line with a *swish* into the water, slicing the moon in two for a moment. He rested the rod on a rock then dipped his green net into the silver water.

Catching the moon was what he loved doing best. He skimmed the net along the shining surface, gathering the hills of lunar highlands and the valley of Mare Tranquillitatis, all within his small net. And when he lifted it, a shimmering catch of diamond droplets showered out of it like a starburst across a frozen sea. Mooncatching... Just when you thought you had it, you lost it.

"You can't catch the moon, you know. I've tried," came a voice from the bulrushes.

River swerved round. There was no one there. Only a soft wind swayed the feathery rush tops.

"I know that," he said to the nowhere person, trying to keep his voice steady. It was one thing expecting something to come out of the water and quite another to find something already out and behind you. He searched the shadows nervously.

"I love the moon, don't you?" said the voice.

It was closer now and River jumped to find a woman sitting on the bank beside him. She hadn't been there a moment ago. She was pale and greyish and she was smiling at the moon's reflection. Her legs waggled to and fro in the water. She wore a long, tattered dress that floated on the silver surface. Tangles of pondweed peeped through its holes.

"I…" River couldn't find another word. He was too surprised.

The woman turned to face him. "Oh!" she said, seeming a little surprised herself. Her watery blue eyes looked kind but otherworldly, as if she came from the moon herself. Strands of her dark hair blew about, though there was no wind. "You can hear me? Hear me words, not just me moanin'?"

River nodded, a bit puzzled by her question. Why wouldn't he be able to hear her?

"Well, that's never happened before. Must have been magic you threw into the pond that made the chimin' sound." She smiled at him. "Always knew you were special. You came with the first snow of winter. To the cottage where music plays. Been lovely, watchin' you fish and grow." She moved her hand gently over his forehead as if to lift his hair. She didn't touch him, but River could feel the cold coming from her fingers. It was a bit odd, but River didn't like to show his discomfort, because of the kind way she looked at him.

"I … I like the moon too," he said, thinking it impolite not to speak.

"I knows you do." She smiled again, this time right into his eyes, then flicked back her head and laughed. "Here! Me pa were always singin' about the moon… *Hey, diddle, diddle, the cat and the fiddle, the cow jumped over the moon!* Know what's up there?" She pointed to the moon. "A cow!" she said and laughed again.

"I don't think so," said River. "They'd have found it, or at least its bones when they were up there."

"When who were up there?"

"The astronauts. You know, the men that went to the moon."

"Strastranauts!" she said. "That be silly as my tomfoolery!"

"No, it's true. Men did go to the moon." River looked at her, puzzled. "Didn't you know?"

"Went to the moon!" said the woman, her eyes like saucers. "How did that happen? Hardly ever took my eyes off it."

How could she not know about the moon landings? He wondered if she came from a travelling theatre and never read the news, or something. Her hooded cloak and puffed sleeves certainly looked theatrical. "Do you live near by?" he asked.

"I live here by," she replied, spinning her finger and leaving a trail of mist. "Used to live o'er yonder at Azakeyle's Inn, but can't get back there, these days."

"You live here, by the pond?" River asked. He'd never heard of anyone living by Bigdeepby Pond. A lot of the villagers were a bit scared of it because it was so deep, and some said it was full of strange creatures. Some even said it was haunted. River hadn't believed the rumours before, but he shivered now and glanced at the woman again.

"I do. Me, three hundred tadpoles, two thousand frogspawn, twelve ducks and a partridge in a pear tree! We all lives here." Her curly smile returned and she

18

splashed a foot in the water. "Not so lucky with the fish tonight," she added, nodding at the fishing line. "You only ever keep the one, don't you? And throw all the others back."

River felt a little uneasy. She must have really been watching him to know that. But she seemed so gentle, so unusual, it didn't bother him as much as it might have done. "We can't eat more than one," he said.

The woman nodded, then pointed to the sky. "Look!" she said, nudging him. A falling star fizzled into the velvet darkness. "Quick, make a wish!"

"A wish…" River's mind went blank. He could only think about how odd she was. Maybe he should ask her straight out who she was and why she was there, but it didn't feel right somehow. She might think it was rude. "I wish…" He sighed and shrugged his shoulders. What he really wanted was for Bettina and the others to stop picking on him, but he wasn't sure this star was big enough for that. He'd need a whole galaxy of wishes.

"'Tis all right," she said. "You can throw the

19

wish back like fish and it'll come to you later when you needs it. Now, here we go... My wish!" She waved her arms grandly. River gasped as sparks flew from her sleeves but they were only moths that fluttered away. "I wish I could go home to me Raphty, buried under our tree! I'd be with him now if it weren't for that GOOD FER NOTHIN' PIRATE!"

Her voice was so loud that River jumped. She didn't seem quite so kind and friendly any more but angry and a little bit scary.

Chapter 2

For a second, River wanted to get his things and go. Then the woman breathed in deep and seemed calm as ripples again.

"Why can't you go home?" he asked after a moment.

"Because I drow—" She clutched her stomach and jiggled about on her skirts. "'Cause I drowned right here," she said finally.

The hair on the back of River's neck prickled. "So, you're a … ghost?"

"Am I?" She thought for a moment. "Suppose I am." A cloud raced over the moon and darkness crept in around them.

21

River gulped. The legends about Bigdeepby Pond were true, after all. He always thought he'd be scared of a ghost. But here he was sitting beside one. Not a moan, not a groan, not a *whoo*, not a *whaa*. And as the moon returned, he realized he wasn't afraid. Not really. Maybe it was only floating sheets with cut-out holes he was scared of. He looked at her pale fingers and noticed for the first time that he could see the grass right through them. She had kind hands, though. He watched her face a moment. She had kind eyes too – when she wasn't shouting about pirates.

Suddenly, the woman shuddered. River's mouth fell open as a fluffy duckling waddled through the side of her skirts. "'Ere! No passin' through! That tickles. Get home to your mother with thee!" She giggled as the squeaking duckling flurried across the pond in zigzags and into the bulrushes.

River bit his lip, then laughed. Scared? No, he had nothing to be scared of. *OK, she's a ghost*, he thought, watching her, *but weren't ghosts people too? Yes,* he decided. She was just a person of the see-through kind, that's all. He smiled to himself.

He'd never known a night like it or anyone like her.

"It's special here," said River, feeling more confident now.

The pale woman nodded and smiled. "Aye, that it be. The story goes this village were once a fairy hill. And see that there Pointer's Peak? They say a giant leaped from it – thinking this 'ere pond were a puddle – and the fairy hill got flattened… Squashing the magic out of it. *Woomph!*"

River laughed.

"Nowadays, only bits and starts of magic pop up 'ere and there," said the woman, sighing. "Reckon that's what happened tonight when you threw those coins in the pond. You woke the magic so you could hear and see me. Not that magic's helped me much. I keeps a-wishin' I could go home to me Raphty. But me bones are still down there. All me treasures and all me bones."

"But why can't you just float, or fly – or whatever ghosts do to move about – to find Raphty?"

She didn't answer for a second. River threw a dandelion into the water and they watched it glide. "Usually you gets to be together again with those you love. No matter how or where you said goodbyes, you can always find a way to them. Together always and evermore, whatever star you follow. 'Tis just me, I can't move on."

River wanted to ask what she meant, but then he saw her glistening eyes and wanted to cheer her up instead. "Would you like to try mooncatching?" He handed her the net but her fingers passed right through it.

"'T'always looks beautiful when you do it," said the woman, shaking her head. "You do it for me."

River nodded and dipped the net into the curve of the mirrored moon. He heard her sigh as she grinned ear to ear. It felt good to see her smile again.

"That's the Crater of Copernicus," he whispered as he scooped its reflection and held it there.

"Caught you, old Copper Knickers!" she cried out, as River swung the net in the air.

Water gushed through
the diamond web and showered
into the pond. A duck quacked
angrily and changed direction,
splashing them with a flurry of wings.
River shook his wet hair and burst
out laughing, hitting the grass with
his hand.

"Used to try mooncatchin' with
a bucket when I were a lass," said
the woman. "What a lark we had!
Bucket's not as pretty as this, though."

River shook the net to watch the
crystal blues and purples fall. "It's
moving," he said, pointing at the
moon's reflection.

"Aye," said the woman. "Sky
sailing, it be. Happen it's off to look at
itself in some faraway river or sea." She
tipped her head. "Your name's River, be
it not?"

25

"How did you know that?"

"Aah." She winked. "A little Boot told me."

"Boot?"

The woman smiled. "Always look for the hidden. I reckons if you try fishin' again, you might find somethin'" – she nodded at the sparkling surface – "special."

Curious, River plunged his net into the pond.

What he pulled out shouldn't have been alive. Glassy eyes and tatty fake fur. Its claws seemed made of wood and the nose looked like velvet. But the moment River laid the little toy badger on the grass, took the hook from its fur and looked into those black eyes, he knew…

It was alive.

"H-hello, you," said River.

The small creature sat up and coughed. Water fizzed through its teeth and it held a paw in the air, as if to tell River to wait. When it had finished coughing up water, it looked River up and down and nodded at him.

River smiled back.

"Hello, Boot," said the woman.

The badger shook itself dry then snuggled up beside her.

"How did you know it was there?" River asked the woman.

"Boot be an old friend." She hovered her hands over the badger's ears a moment. River could see the badger's matted fur through her transparent fingers. Boot looked cross and wiggled to get her hands away. She smiled at him and said quickly, "He drowned-ed not long after me. Reckon some pirate kicked him in." Boot finally shook her hands away, gave her a don't-do-that-again look, then had a good scratch. "He needs a bit of love, is all." She stroked his ears without touching them, as she had River's head, and sighed. "Someone should take him home for keeps."

River looked at her funny smile and then at Boot. Reaching out, he patted the little badger. He was warm despite the pond water and the cold night. "You want to come home with me?" he whispered. Boot wriggled his neck under River's hand for more stroking, and River took that as a yes. River's eyes stung suddenly – he'd wanted a friend for a long time. "Thank you," he said.

The woman smiled. "Time for you to be a-headin' home. Your ma will be wonderin' where yous got to. And happen you've got schoolin' tomorrow. There be other times for a-talkin'."

"Yeah," said River, knowing it was almost bedtime. "I should go now." Back home he could think things through. Maybe by morning he'd realize it had all been a dream, he thought, and felt a little sad.

Getting up to gather his things he looked back at the strange woman with the kind eyes, smiling at him. He stopped a moment then asked, "Will you be here tomorrow night?"

"I be 'ere every night. Only usually no one knows it," said the woman. She looked into the little badger's eyes and told him, "Take good care of River now and bring him back tomorrow night."

River took the little badger carefully and smiled. "We'll see you tomorrow."

"Good," said the woman. "Now be off with you. I got some moanin' to do. 'Tis hard work bein' a spook."

River walked towards the cottages with Boot on his shoulder. At the edge of the rushes, he turned back to wave at the ghost and realized he didn't even know her name.

River and Boot talked all the way home. A short walk across the square to the second lane on the right. They had so much in common. They both loved the night; they both loved the quiet when the world was sleeping; and they both loved the moon. River told Boot how he liked to fish but mostly he loved mooncatching when the moon was full, when the biggest fish were dizzy from its beauty and came out of their deepest hiding places.

Boot knew all about this – Boot knew many things – and had sometimes caught fish snacks this way himself as they leaped out of the water, moonstruck.

When they reached River's cottage on the corner, the moon shone on the thatched roof. River scraped his trainers on the doorstep and took pondweed from Boot's fur before stepping through the back door. Puddles of mud and pond water followed the little badger across the kitchen floor anyway. After reassuring Boot that a fluffy towel was your friend and not a flying otter, River put him to dry on the kitchen radiator and said goodnight.

*Not all friendships start
with a pond rescue
and a night on a radiator.
But this one did.*

Chapter 3

"**B**ye, Mum!" called River, before closing the front door. In the milky morning sunlight, he left his cottage on the corner and crossed over to the village square. The bulrushes by Bigdeepby Pond waved sleepily as he went by. He breathed in their spring scents before hurrying on, past the lanes and huddled shops.

Everyone was talking about it on their way to school – the wailing from Bigdeepby Pond.

"Did you hear the noises from the pond last night?" River heard Bettina ask Casey as he passed the school railings. Bettina gave River more chills than a ghost ever could, but at the mention of noises he kneeled behind a tree to listen, pretending to tie his shoelace.

"Yeah, so creepy," said Casey, shuddering. "I told Dad, but he just pretended it wasn't happening."

"Mum says it's got to be the ghost of that drowned woman who died in the pond hundreds of years ago. People say they see her sometimes – late at night – but I don't think that's true. Although there is some weird stuff by that pond. Anyway, no one's ever actually heard her before."

River stood up and moved a little closer. They had to be talking about the woman he'd met, didn't they?

Bettina looked up then and saw River. "Hello, little River. Listening to our conversation, are you?"

River blushed. Bettina tugged his backpack strap as he moved away, making him stumble. Anger bubbled inside him as he straightened up, pretending not to care.

"He's so weird," said Casey, pushing past River. "He's not coming to your party on Sunday, is he?"

"No way!" said Bettina. "He'd make a good scarecrow, though. Keep the birds off the buffet."

Casey howled with laughter as they stepped through the gate and into the school yard.

"They think they're funny but they're not," whispered River, slipping his hand through the zip of his backpack to feel Boot's fur.

Boot knew all about these things, and had met that sort himself. Always posing about, thinking they're handsome and clever and laughing at his striped snout and wobbly underbelly. But foxes weren't all that. Just red dogs with fluffy tails dipped in chalk.

"Yeah," whispered River, turning to see if anyone had noticed his talking backpack.

Some folk don't like it when you're different, Boot went on. *And what a funny place the world would be if everyone was the same and no one had a striped snout or wobbly underbelly.*

River felt a little less alone as he made his way to his seat in the classroom. Bettina was sitting on a desk by the window, loudly telling everyone about the presents she had demanded for her birthday. River took out his schoolbooks, glancing towards the window at the same time, and got a fright when Fergus Fuggle, the school caretaker, suddenly appeared on the other side of the glass. He gave a spooky wail, making everyone jump. They all laughed when they saw it was only Fergus. He was always playing pranks that everyone else thought hilarious, but River wasn't so sure. Fergus was making fun of the ghost he had just met. And there was nothing hilarious about that.

Wailing again, Fergus squeezed a sponge over his head, the bubbles running over his teeth, and made a gargling, drowning noise.

Everyone laughed except River.

Bettina knocked on the glass. "You're creepy enough without pretending to be a ghost."

"Quiet down, everyone!" said Miss Marland, carrying books into the classroom.

Fergus ducked out of sight, his bucket clattering.

Voices sank to a hush as twenty pairs of eyes watched a small dark-haired girl follow their teacher in. The girl looked across the room. River gulped when her brown eyes met his. She gave him a friendly smile and he looked away shyly, then instantly wished he'd smiled back.

"Now, this is Kaleisha," Miss Marland went on. "She's just moved to the village. So let's give her a lovely welcome to our school. Can everyone say, *Hello, Kaleisha*?"

"Hello, Kaleisha," came the singsong reply.

"Hello," said Kaleisha.

Miss Marland smiled and showed her to a desk two rows behind River.

"Did you hear the noises at the pond last night, miss?" asked Bettina.

"I hear noises all day long. *Please, miss, I've no pen! Please, miss, my goldfish ate my homework! Please, miss, my homework ate the dog!*" Everyone laughed. "Yes, I heard the wailing last night too. It's nothing for you to worry about. I suspect it's just old Moanie. A poor lost soul who can't find peace, or so the legend goes. Plenty of people have seen her, and some have heard her, but not for a long time. That's supposed to be part of her curse, poor love, never to be heard so she can't ask for her last wish to be granted and be at peace. Maybe her luck is changing, or perhaps there was some magic in the air last night."

There was a hush in the room. "What happened to her?" asked Casey, chewing the end of her plait nervously.

"Well." Miss Marland hesitated and then said, "They say she drowned in the pond."

Everyone in class gasped. Bettina gave Casey a knowing nod: *I told you so.*

"But it's all just legend," Miss Marland said quickly. "Probably the wailing was foxes, or some other creature. Or maybe she was a teacher whose entire class was eaten by a homework-gulping goldfish." Miss Marland smiled, trying to lighten the mood in the room.

Nervous giggles rippled around the classroom.

"Did the Crackenlurk eat her bones, miss?" asked Casey with glee.

"Now *that* monster's real," said Bettina. "'Cause so many pets go missing."

River had heard about the missing pets too. There were stories that a swamp creature that no one had seen, known as the Crackenlurk, had gobbled them up. Bigdeepby was full of stories. But as his mum had once said, legends run away with themselves sometimes and maybe the pets had too.

"OK, that's enough legends for today," said Miss Marland, looking round at the anxious faces in the class.

River was disappointed. He'd wanted to ask more about Moanie and her last wish. Tonight, he and Boot would see Moanie again and maybe then he'd get the answers to some of his questions. Maybe they would do some mooncatching too.

River smiled thinking about it. He turned to face the front where Miss Marland was writing on the whiteboard. The soft squeak of the pen reminded him of the sounds of ducklings settling at night. The taps of Miss Marland's feet were bulrushes snapping.

If Moanie needed help and had something to say, he would listen. He wanted to talk to Boot about it but there was no time now. The class had to read out loud. River's stomach fluttered as it came closer to his turn. But then he felt a furry snout on his leg, and saw the badger peeking out of his bag.

River breathed in deep. Somehow, with Boot beside him, reading out loud didn't seem so bad.

Just before the bell rang, Bettina's hand shot up. "Can I hand out invitations for my pool party, miss?" she asked.

"As long as everyone gets one," said Miss Marland.

Bettina walked along the aisles placing gold envelopes on desks. River packed his pencil case into the side of his backpack and saw Boot snoozing under the flap.

"Here's one for you, Kaleisha," said Bettina. "I had some extra." River saw Miss Marland nod at Bettina as if she was doing a nice thing. "And one for you, River," Bettina added loudly.

But when Miss Marland turned to wipe the whiteboard, Bettina tapped an envelope on his head and put it on another desk. He rubbed his hair and looked away, certain she was smirking at him. His cheeks burned red and he hoped more than anything that she hadn't noticed. He didn't want to go to her stupid party anyway.

"Don't forget your recycling project for tomorrow," called Miss Marland as the bell rang.

The room filled with chatter and scraping chairs as everyone headed for the door.

Before leaving, River saw Kaleisha drop something gold into the bin. She grinned at him as she did it.

River smiled. Maybe he'd found a friend.

"Friends are like the sun,"
said a wise goose.
"When they meet a storm cloud,
they make a rainbow."

Chapter 4

Moths circled the window as River tapped on the glass. His mum was playing cello indoors. He waved his green net at her and she waved back, smiling, as he set off down the path. The village clock clanged the hour, scattering bats from its tower. It was time for his visit to the pond.

The air was full of night scents as River hurried out of the gate and ran over cobblestones. Behind glowing windows, the villagers of Bigdeepby had their TVs and music on loud, and River wondered if it was to drown out any more ghostly noises coming from the pond.

Boot spotted Moanie before River did. She was sitting on a low branch of a tree, silhouetted in the moonlight, arms waving like an opera singer. Her eyes lit up on seeing them and she drifted down to the pond. "Moths told me you were a-comin'," she said and air-patted the grass beside her.

"Moanie…" River said hesitantly, kneeling down as she dipped her legs in the water.

"Ah, so you've learned my name. They likes to call me Moanie. Can't blame 'em. Like a good moan when I'm bored, but it's been a long time since anyone other than the ducks and the fishes was able to hear me. Maybe there's magic in the air this year. My real name's Mona. Mona Brightly." Boot stepped out of the backpack and wriggled between them. "Snuggle-boots," Mona said and air-tickled Boot's ears.

"I've been thinking," said River, watching them. "Could someone help you to get home to Raphty?"

"That be like catchin' the moon – impossible," Mona said, shaking her head. "'Tis too late to get me and Raphty together. Us being dead 'n'all." She watched her feet twinkling underwater.

River thought of his nanna who had told him she'd always be with him. He looked at the stars and felt it was true. "But you said we all got to be with the ones we loved, that it was just you who couldn't move on," he said. "Can't I help you? You should meet him again."

"What a comfort you be, River," said Mona with a small smile. Mosquitoes buzzed through her, turning into ice-blue sparkles. "'Tis my greatest dream to be with Raphty again. I'll never truly be at peace until our bones are resting together in the home we loved, under the tree we planted."

"But you said it didn't matter where we say goodbye. That we can find our way to our loved ones. So why can't you just go to Raphty now and forget your bones?"

"Hmm," said Mona. She got to her feet and pointed to the church at the other end of the village. "See that steeple? How about I goes there and wakeys up folks with a bit of bell ringin'?"

Before he could answer, Mona was gliding through bulrushes and onto the square. "Wait!" he called, running after her.

Mona whizzed past his cottage and up the lane. She whooshed across hedges and looped an arch into the churchyard. Moths and leaves swirled after her as she sped to the church and flew up its walls.

"*Woohoo!*" she cried, pirouetting on a gargoyle's head, halfway up the steeple. She leaped to a ledge below the bell tower. "You can see *everythin's* up here! 'Tis ... beautificent! You should take a look!"

"I-I-I'm OK down here, thanks," called River.

"Gets uppity!" she told her leg, trying to stretch it over a turret. Suddenly she gripped the stone wall. "Uh oh!" she sang, and River watched in horror as Mona was dragged down the steeple, sparks flying.

"Mona?" called River.

"YES?" she yelled, stopping, then ... "NOOOOO!" With a *swish*, she catapulted backwards, zooming past River. She crackled over thatched roofs, back along his lane. Straw flying and weathervanes spinning.

"MONA!" shouted River, sprinting to the pond

as she tunnelled through reeds that snapped like firecrackers.

"WHOA!" came Mona's voice followed by an enormous splash.

River raced through the rushes to the water's edge, his heart pounding. Circles grew across the surface but Mona was nowhere to be seen.

"Mona!" called River, falling to his knees. He dipped his head underwater and opened his eyes. All he could see below was darkness. Was she hurt? Had she gone for ever? Suddenly a hand shot towards him through the water. River gasped and sucked in a mouthful of pond water.

"Murky, in't it?" said Mona, laughing as she bounced up from the pond.

River groaned in relief, and shook water from his head, spluttering.

"Just wanteds to show you what would happen, that's all!" she said. "Them bones of mine always bring me back. I don't knows why. Doesn't seem to me that all ghosts are tethered to their bones. 'Tis just me, unlucky diddler! And ghosts can't touch their own bones, see, so I can't even carry 'em to me Raphty." Mona sighed. "I be stuck in this 'ere village like a dandelion. I bet it's somethin' to do with that ROTTEN RASCAL PIRATE!" At the sound of her voice, ducks leaped from the water in fright and vanished into the reeds.

"Who be this … who was this pirate?" asked River.

"Dashbuckle Fearless," she said, shuddering. She leaned towards him, speaking low. "See, long ago me pa Azakeyle were a pirate but he stopped his no-goodery and opened an inn. People came from miles for a taste of his brews. His most famous was supposed to make folks live longer. And Pa named it after the moon – the Lunalixir! Full of fruit, it be, which made me pa laugh. An innkeeper sellin' a fruit drink. It were all health, he said. Health and happiness, that's what makes you live long. But it made him a fortune.

"When Pa died, rumour spread I hads a treasure chest of gold coins and a magical Lunalixir that made you live for ever! It was said it could even brung you back to life." Mona laughed. River laughed too, until the light dimmed in Mona's eyes.

"But that's when Dashbuckle came a-creepin'. That no good thievin' pirate. He and me pa had been piratin' together back before Pa gave it all up. Dashbuckle thought Pa owed him. Said he'd cart me off to his pirate ship and make me walk the plank if I didn't brings 'im me treasure and the Lunalixir! So, I told the pirate me treasure and the Lunalixir be in a box in Drippydrop Cave by a stalagmite what looked like a hat. And when he be gone, I ran to the inn to get me treasure, me hat and me cloak and I followed the moon the whole night long."

She tossed her cloak over her shoulder and strode through a trail of fireflies. "'Till I reached this 'ere pond." She hovered above the water, the fireflies dancing about her. "So tired I be, I fell asleep."

"Did the pirate come after you?"

"Oh, I'd a creepity feelin' he were a-followin'," Mona said. "Well, that thought waked me up. So I tried hidin' me treasure in the rushes 'ere. 'Twas then I heard a noise!" River gasped as she waved her arms frantically. "Somethin' shoved me from behind. I tooks a tumble, hit me head on a rock and fell in the pond, with me treasure!" She dropped towards the water. River tried to grab her but his hand slipped right through. Mona stopped herself suddenly and swirled back beside him. "'Tweren't no reeds what pushed me. Oh, no. Me thinks … 'twere that pirate."

"Dashbuckle Fearless," whispered River and shivered as a fish snapped a fly from the surface.

"Aye," said Mona, "but don't worry 'bout him, for he be long deaded and gone."

River understood why Mona was so angry with the pirate. Wondering how he could help, he watched a falling star leap between trees. "Another wish!" he said. "I could use it to wish your bones home to Raphty."

Mona pulled a funny face. "Wishes be tricky as fishes, but 'tis worth a try."

She sounded doubtful so River said, "Or I could throw some coins into the pond. I did that yesterday for good luck and you appeared." River remembered the ringing sound from the pond when the coins struck something on the bottom.

"Aye," said Mona, lifting an eyebrow. "A chimin' woked us from our nod, Boot and me. And then you were able to see us and hear us speak. It's been a long time since that's happened." River watched her tap her lips and thought about how the people of Bigdeepby had been able to hear Mona's wailing for once. "Your coins tip-tapped on an old bell that lay besides us, in the Bigdeepby down there. P'rhaps it be a magic bell."

River's eyes opened wide. "If we throw in another coin, we could wish for the magic to bring up your bones and then I could take them to wherever Raphty is."

Digging through his pockets River found a fuzzy sweet and several stones. "I don't have any more coins, but here's three pebbles," he said, holding them up. "We could try these."

Mona gasped at them as though they were jewels. "Wait," she said. "I will say words to giddy-up the magic."

"You know magic?"

"If strastranauts can hop to the moon, ain't we all magic?" said Mona. She put on her hood, waved her hands over her face and swept her arms across the pond. Boot's belly wobbled from laughing but

River shook his head at him. "Hibble, bibble, boo and bubble ... now throw!"

River slung the first pebble in the water.

Glup!

"Bone's a-hop and pirate's trouble!" called Mona.

River threw in the second one.

Glup!

"Wait, did I say pirate's trouble?" asked Mona. "I meant to say, *be no trouble*."

"You said pirate's trouble!" said River. "Take it back! Take it back!"

"Pirate's trouble, bring it back!" cried Mona, sweeping her arms and making River jump so the last pebble leaped from his hand. It flew through the air and landed – *glup!* – in the pond.

"NO!" River cried, horrified she might just have wished the pirate back. "*Take it back*, not *bring it back!*"

"I says take it back, I be sure I did," said Mona, biting her lip. "Anyways," she added, "there be no such thing as magi—"

Chu-uy-ung!

River's blood turned cold.

Chu-uy-ung!

"And they be only words…" Mona's voice faded to a whisper.

Chu-uy-ung!

Bubbles rose from the water and crossed to the opposite side of the pond, where the swamp was. Across its bank, leaves and dust blasted a trail into the reeds. Crackles and snaps sped away until they could hear no more.

"Only words," said River, facing the swamp. "But all the wrong ones." His hair stood on end and his mouth went dry. "A-any idea where Dashbuckle died?"

Mona looked at him with fear in her eyes. "Don't know. We be talkin' three hundred years ago. He likely, most probably-definitelys died … far away. Dashbuckle wouldn't want to be a-hangin' about here."

The ground trembled and more sounds came from the far side of the swamp.

GLUG! FIZZ! BLURPH!

"I reckons he's REALLY far, far away," shouted Mona, shooing with her hand, as if trying to convince the magic to move on.

But it was too late. From the swamp, came the cry of something wild.

BWUAAAAAAAAAAAAK!

"What was that?" asked River.

"Whatever that be," said Mona, drifting backwards, her arm pointing to the nearby boglands beyond the swamp, "went thataway."

Beware of the thataways.
It might be the thisaways.
Only your heart knows the rightaways
on your long road ahead.

Chapter 5

Chu-uy-ung! Chu-uy-ung! Chu-uy-ung!
  "… Pirate's trouble, bring it back!"
BWUAAAAAAAAAAAK!

Dashbuckle rose up through the swamp with a yell. He blinked when he found himself covered in stinking mud, staring up at an almost full moon.

The last thing he remembered was diving into the pond after that pirate girl's – Mina? Miza? – treasure. If only he'd noticed her holding it before he pushed her in.

No, he thought. That wasn't quite the last thing he remembered. With his final watery breath, he'd floated to the surface of the pond, where something huge had waited. The thing had dragged him away to this swamp, where he'd dreamed that centuries of stars had sailed by.

And now he was awake again. He sat upright and looked around him at muddy puddles and spiky tufts of grass. Then he looked down at his legs, *through* his legs, at oozing mud beneath him. He must be a ghost, he realized. *Well, at least I can fly to me treasure faster*, he thought. He launched himself into the air but fell back down again instantly. He could only air-walk above the ground, at the height of the daisies.

"ARGH!" he snarled, hoping the floaty-flying would come with practice. "So, where be me bones?"

PLOFF! A frog leaped from a puddle beside him and he yelped to find a skeleton half-covered in mud. On its skull lay a semi-transparent ghostly three-cornered hat.

"Hat o'mine!" said Dashbuckle, grinning as he scooped it out of swamp-gloop. He patted it onto his ghost-head, its peacock feather bouncing. "Now, where be that pond with me treasure?" He staggered about, searching and sniffing until he

reached an opening in
the reeds. He could see
no pond, only boglands,
which spluttered and
hissed about him
like sleeping giants.

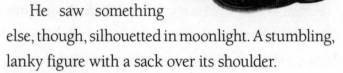

He saw something
else, though, silhouetted in moonlight. A stumbling,
lanky figure with a sack over its shoulder.

FWHIZZ!

"BOG GAS!" screamed the figure as a fountain
of fire lit the night sky behind him. "Th-that
were close!" he told the screeching swamp birds,
then laughed. And as orange flames shrunk and
dimmed, he shuffled closer to Dashbuckle. "How
do? I'm Fergus. Been diggin' peat in bog. Lost yer
ship, 'ave yer?" Fergus snorted. "No sea round
'ere! Swamp ahoy!"

"'Tis a pond I be lookin' for!" Dashbuckle
growled. "POOOND!"

"Hey, are you … are you a … ghost?" Fergus's
voice shook.

"Aye, that I be, and I be a-hauntin' ye if ye

don't tell me where the pond is."

Fergus pointed a trembling finger at the trail to the village. "This w-w-way around the swamp," he stuttered, then screamed as Dashbuckle edged closer, and his ghostly chill fell all around him.

"You better be tellin' the truth!" barked Dashbuckle. "In a hurry I be! When I gets me treasure and the Lunalixir to brings me back to life for ever, I be sailin' the six seas afar!"

"In't it *seven* seas?"

"Aye, fishface, seven it be! But there's one I avoid 'cause of a certain sea monster. NOT that I be afraid of no sea monsters, mind!"

Fergus shook his head. "Did you say that you were lookin' for treasure? 'Cause I likes treasure."

"The treasure be mine," Dashbuckle roared.

Fergus scratched his head, thinking. "Yeah, but an important pirate like you will need … an assisty-ant. And me 'ere can be that assisty-ant, if you swapsies for some of your treasure."

Dashbuckle stared at the lanky lad for a second. He didn't look very useful but Dashbuckle did like the idea of an assistant. Until he could find the Lunalixir he was stuck as a ghost. And ghosts couldn't touch anything. "Ye can help me, and in exchange I won't haunt ye for the rest of yer squid-squawkin' life. Do we have a deal?"

Fergus nodded, eyes wide with fear.

"Get a move on, then, or I'll feed ye to a flock of sharkadiles!" said Dashbuckle, pressing close to Fergus and blasting icy breath over him.

"Not if the Crackenlurk eats us first," squeaked Fergus. "We're right in the middle of its swamp."

"Yackenyurk!" mimicked Dashbuckle then gulped, remembering his ma's tales of magical creatures that could gobble up ghosts. What if it was a cousin of a sea serpent with land legs? He watched Fergus look nervously about, shaking frost from his clothes. Moments later, the nincompoop lad tumbled face-first into the swamp. "Floppin' fishface," growled Dashbuckle. "I haven't got all night. Takes us the other way, if we be … you be scared of this Yackenyurk." With slow, squishy steps they skirted around the swamp.

And then they heard it. A laugh that rose through the summer night, shaking Dashbuckle's cold heart into a thousand stars.

It could be only one. He remembered that very laugh. It could be only Mina!

Dashbuckle shook his fists at the sea-greens and purples that flimmered across the sky. Rage washed over him like a rising sea. He was close to his treasure now, but Mindy wouldn't let him have it without a fight.

"'Tis that pirate's daughter whose treasure I be after!" he said as a wild wind blew about him.

"That'll be Moanie," said Fergus, his eyes wide on his muddy face. "Her what drowned in the pond..."

Dashbuckle picked a ghost-earwig from his boot, slurped it up and cackled. Why, Moeena would be a pushover now, her being a ghost and all. "Me new life and fortune awaits!" said Dashbuckle, blasting Fergus's face with kipper-breath. "And ye, ye blubberin' blobfish, be just the lad to digs me treasure from the pond's bottom."

"From village pond's bottom?" said Fergus.

"Aye!"

"Bigdeepby Pond's bottom?"

"Aye! Aye!"

"The Big Deep's bottom?"

"Aye! Aye! Aye!" snarled Dashbuckle, freezing Fergus so his hair stood on end.

"They don't call it the Big Deep for nuffin'," squealed Fergus, through chattering teeth.

"Are you goin' to be useful or am I goin' to be freezin' you with my ghost breath for all eternity?"

Fergus gulped, and Dashbuckle smiled. *Silly sea-slug lad*, he thought. *I won't be a ghost after I've drunk the Lunalixir. Still, no need to remind Fergus of that.* "Now, about this pond. Has ye a ladder?"

"Yeah," said Fergus, clutching his spade. "I

does window cleanin's an' odd jobs."

"'Ere be an odd job for ye!" said Dashbuckle. "Run to that pond, take a deep breath, jump down yer ladder and DIG!"

"No fank you," said Fergus.

"Run an' jumps be good for yers." Dashbuckle smirked, his eyes gleaming gold.

"Only if you g-g-gives us some of your treasure," said Fergus.

"I'll give yer some of me treasure," said Dashbuckle, then whispered down his sleeve, "And then I'll takes it back!"

"Never hand a hope balloon to someone with a pin," said a wise clown. "Never hug a balloon," said a wise hedgehog. "They're so dramatic."

Chapter 6

"'Twas only a whirlwind," said Mona, her skirts brushing bulrush fluff from the grass in the moonlight. "I'm not a magic saucer."

River knew she meant sorcerer but didn't like to say. He stood on a fallen tree, staring at the swamp, hoping nothing was there. "But what you said, and the yell that came after... It could have been the pirate."

"No, no," said Mona, sitting back by the pond, looking less worried. "'Twere a toad that hopped off to the boglands. Awful yellers, them toads."

River wasn't so sure. He listened all about, but he couldn't hear anything. He decided to forget about it for the moment. If the pirate was back, it wouldn't be long before he found the pond and Mona's treasure. River would need to act fast if he was going to help move her bones and treasure, or her last wishes would never come true. She'd never rest beside her Raphty. It was a shame the magic hadn't worked to bring her bones out of the water.

"I'll think of some way to get your bones," said River. "And your treasure."

"And take them back home to Raphty with me?"

"Yes," said River. "If you show me where you lived."

Mona flung herself backwards, her hands on her heart. "The place where I lived!" she said. "After all these years of bein' stuck here. Can't believe I might see Dinglebeck again!" She smiled at the stars. "A night-fisher boy. A mooncatcher." She looked at him with soft eyes. "We'd a feelin' you'd be the one to rescue me. Mooncatchers can change anythin'."

The pond gleamed with colour and Mona gasped, pointing to the sky. A glimmer of green hung like a curtain on a washing line of stars.

"'Tis a sign everythin's goin' to be all right!"

"Aurora Borealis!" said River.

"Roarer Borin' Alice," whispered Mona. "A beautiforius name."

River tried not to laugh. The lights swayed, then rippled into nothingness. It felt good having someone believe in him. His mum believed in him, and quite a few ducks and frogs thought he was pretty funny, but friends had been hard to find in Bigdeepby. He glanced at Boot, then looked back at the water. "The thing is," he said, "I don't know how I'm going to reach the bottom of the pond."

"They don't call it the Big Deep for nothin'," said Mona, sitting up. "I can swim there but can't dig up me own bones, not even lift them. I'd have stopped trying after three hundred years but it made Boot laugh so."

"I can swim *and* dig," said River.

"Promise you won't!" Mona gripped his arm. "There be weeds and whirls what tugs you under." Her worried eyes searched his face.

"I promise," he said.

Boot said he was a swimmer too, but after past experiences he'd rather not. He was rather good at digging, though. If only his old friend Hyper the hippopotamus, circus escapee, was around. After taking out the fishes, he could sit in the pond and empty it in one go!

"If onlys," Mona said. "The world be full of 'em! If only there weren't no pirates, for one." A crack came from behind and they turned to look. Long moon shadows crept from the pond rushes and swayed as River watched them. He shivered even though the night was warm, and Boot stuck his nose in the air and sniffed.

"Happen it were a toad," said Mona, patting Boot's fur. "Eaten too many creakhoppers. Gettin' fat." Boot gave her a glare. "The toad. Not you, Boot."

They sat in silence for a while, listening to the sounds of the pond. After a bit River opened his bait box, fastened eggy breadcrumbs to a hook then cast his line in the water and waited for the fish. He took the little green net and swished it to and fro, through reflections of moon craters. From the corner of his eye, he caught Mona staring back along the jagged reeds and beyond the upturned tree. Thoughts of the pirate came creeping back.

"We need a plan," he said, hugging his legs, "before it's too late."

"Aye," said Mona, watching Boot creep to the rushes and sniff. "We be needin' a plan ... and soon."

A wise woman once said,
"Plans are maps for wishes."
A wise Boot once said,
"Nets are curtains for fishes."
A wise fish said nothing.

Chapter 7

The next morning, when River was walking to school, a girl appeared from one of the cottages just ahead of him. It was Kaleisha. Remembering how she'd smiled at him when she'd thrown Bettina's invitation in the bin, River walked faster to catch up with her, his feet pattering on cobblestones.

"Hi," she said.

"Hi," he said, feeling suddenly shy. He wanted to smile at her but kept his eyes on his feet instead. "So, you just moved here?" he asked the ground.

"Yeah," said Kaleisha, her plaits flying as she pointed at one of the cottages behind them.

"That's where we live, me and my dad."

"Doesn't your mum live with you?" River couldn't believe the words had actually left his head and wished he could fall into a hole as big as his mouth.

Kaleisha didn't seem to mind. "Sort of," she said. "She died but she's in an urn in the living room, next to her lava lamp."

"Oh, I'm sorry," said River. He hoped it didn't sound like he was sorry that she had a lava lamp. "Did she like her lava lamp a lot, then?"

"Yeah, she loved it," said Kaleisha. "She said it was like looking at the universe. You know, those blobby things coming apart and back together. Mum said it was calming." Kaleisha turned to look at him. "I talk to her sometimes," she said. "Tell her what I'm doing and stuff."

"That's…" River paused. He didn't know what to say. He wanted to say, *That's lovely*, but it didn't seem enough. Then: "STOP!" he shouted, holding her back.

"What?" cried Kaleisha.

"You nearly stood on a bogsmoggle." He

pointed to a beetle, scuttling over cobbles. "If you crush them, they stink. Don't think you'd want that on your shoe all day."

"No," said Kaleisha. "Thanks." They walked on as the beetle waddled behind a basket of logs. "A smogglebog."

"Sort of," said River. "Bogsmoggle." He smiled. Smogglebog sounded much nicer.

As they left the square, they talked about some of the other weird things in the village. Kaleisha had seen the stone well on fire but had found the flames were only orange webs flickering in sunlight. River remembered being fooled by the

webs too. He told her they were made by ladybird spiders. As school came into sight, Kaleisha pointed out an anthill, between two trees, that looked like a grinning goblin.

"Its face changes depending on the weather. Smiling means it'll be sunny all day," River told her. "You should see it when it's going to rain. Talk about grumpy!"

"Like the faces of everyone in class if I'd got stinky bogsmoggle goo on my shoes?" said Kaleisha.

"Yeah!" said River, laughing. Kaleisha laughed too, though as they got nearer to the school, River could feel his happiness fading. Another day of Bettina picking on him. When they reached the school gate, Kaleisha was the only one still grinning.

Miss Marland was late. River took out his recycling project and lifted the lid of the shoe box it was in to peek inside. It had taken him ages, and he felt quite proud of it. It was the moon over Bigdeepby Pond made out of cardboard, with moving parts, a starry sky and everything. He smiled, thinking of Mona. Then his smile turned to a frown. He still hadn't worked out how to get her bones from the bottom of the pond.

He looked outside and watched a wind sweep downhill through grasses like a kid rolling through snow. His brain was whirring. Mona had said the pond was too dangerous to dive into, but what if there was no water in it? Then he could just walk over to the bones. Though … what would they do with all the pond creatures? River sighed. That wasn't even the biggest problem. How could you drain a pond as deep as Bigdeepby?

"Made cardboard shoes, have you, little River?" called Bettina from where she was sitting on her desk, interrupting his thoughts. "They're so in! Lucky for you as you can't afford decent trainers." Her friends laughed, and Casey snatched the shoe box from his desk, holding it high. River's chair clattered to the floor as he jumped to reach it.

"Give it back!" shouted River as it was handed to Bettina. Her friends gathered round, laughing as he tried to push through them.

"Give it to him!" came Kaleisha's voice behind them.

Bettina rounded on her. "Who d'you think you're talking to?"

Kaleisha's lip trembled slightly, but bravely she said, "I'm talking to you, Bettina. Give that back to River."

Bettina took a step closer to her. "And what if I don't want to?"

Kaleisha gulped.

Luckily, at that moment, Miss Marland burst into the classroom. "What's going on?" she asked.

"Just checking out River's project, miss," said Bettina, sliding the shoe box back onto his desk.

"Really?" said Miss Marland sharply. "I hope you're being kind, Bettina." She gave River a concerned glance. "I'm really excited to see your project. Let's take a look at it first."

He nodded but could feel his heart racing as he lifted a shape from the box. Two pencils, with tin-foil stars on top, were placed either side of a cardboard moon and sky. It stood on driftwood, painted to look like a cloud. Paper was rolled around each of the pencils and threaded through slits on each side of the moon. Gasps came from all around except from Bettina and her friends.

"It's beautiful, River," said Miss Marland. "Can you tell us all about it?"

"It's a sky theatre, miss," he said. "I made it from cardboard." He could feel all eyes on him and his ears were burning. "It's called Mooncatcher." Bettina and Casey snorted and he pretended not to care. He showed Miss Marland how to roll the paper by turning a pencil, then let her try.

Wows whispered along the desks as a starry sky slid across the cardboard moon, turning it into a crescent. Someone behind River clapped and others joined in until Bettina coughed, which made them all stop.

"Oh!" said Miss Marland, her smile vanishing. "It seems to be stuck."

River took the little theatre and twisted the pencils back and forth, when the whole thing suddenly fell to pieces. All the throwing about had loosened everything from their holes.

Laughter burst out around him, with Bettina's

donkey bray the loudest.

Miss Marland told the class to be quiet. "Well, what an amazing idea, River!" she said, trying to cheer him up. "The sky catches the moon. Let's hope you can fix your Mooncatcher soon."

"That moon caught a meteorite," sneered Bettina and Miss Marland gave her a stern look.

River wanted to yell, twist a pencil and make Bettina and her crew disappear behind a cardboard moon. But that wasn't going to happen. Putting the broken theatre back in the box, he could see Bettina's grin from the corner of his eye and felt his face flush with anger. The hours he'd spent making this project and she'd destroyed it in seconds. Why did she get away with everything?

"First hand up goes next," said Miss Marland.

"Me, miss, me!" called Bettina, smacking Casey's hand down.

"OK, Bettina," said Miss Marland, sighing. "Show us what you've made."

Bettina stuck her nose in the air as she took out her model made from used cardboard and plastic pots.

"So cool!" said Casey. "It's your party."

"Yeah, my birthday pool party," said Bettina, beaming. "And how everything's going to look." River wanted to say it looked like a squirrel had attacked a cereal packet but didn't.

She pointed out details to the class with her little finger. Plastic wrap and an ice-cream tub were her freshwater pool. And when she showed her two floating peacock seats made from yoghurt pots, River thought she actually sounded like a peacock … underwater. Bettina's friends *ooh*-ed and *aah*-ed as she babbled on. "We'll be shopping in Paris for the weekend but will arrive for the party in an ice-cream helicopter. Vans are so last year. There'll be a giant inflatable flamingo for bouncing, a slide and—"

"Thank you, Bettina," said Miss Marland. "That's fascinating. I'm sure everyone will have a lovely time at your party. Time to give someone else a turn now."

Bettina pulled a face but didn't say anything. She thought turns were taking a spin in her limo, thought River. He hoped her party was a disaster.

He knew that was mean, but Bettina was mean all the time. Maybe the party would be invaded by a load of ducks, dancing under her disco sprinklers.

Boot said he used to be friends with a few ducks, all of whom were great divers, but they'd fallen out over a cheese sandwich.

River patted the little badger's head and said he knew all about difficult ducks.

He wasn't thinking about Boot, though. He was thinking about frogs back-flipping on Bettina's giant bouncy flamingo and ducks dancing under disco sprinklers. What if he could send all the pond life to Bettina's pool party? If the pond creatures settled in Bettina's freshwater pool, he wouldn't need to worry about harming

any of them. Then all he would have to do was work out how to drain the water from the pond. He felt excited.

He couldn't wait to tell Mona about his plan tonight.

"What goes around
comes around,"
said the hen to the fox who
caught his own tail.

Chapter 8

River had a three-point plan. Under torchlight he drew pictures in the mud to show Mona the whole idea.

Point One: put the pond life into Bettina Murkhart's massive pool. Bettina was a bully. Adding nature to her freshwater pool didn't really count as being horrible.

Boot agreed and said she might even get on well with pond life because she looked like a frog.

Point Two: drain the pond.

This point had caused River some problems until he'd spotted the sign for the farmers' market fair, happening just outside the village this weekend. And what did a farmers' market have? Lots of animals. And what did lots of animals need? Lots of water. Buckets and troughs of it. The farmers might not drain the whole pond, but they'd lower the water a bit. River did have some doubts about this part of the plan, but he couldn't think of a better one, so he was going with it for now.

Moving the farmers' market to the village square right beside the pond would be easy, he told Mona. Just a case of changing a few arrows on a sign or two.

Boot also saw its brilliance and volunteered for sign-flipping duty immediately.

Point Three: walk to the bottom of the pond and dig up Mona's bones and treasure.

"What do you think?" asked River.

"'Tis a wonderment to behold!" said Mona, clasping her hands. "And me thinks 'twill work!"

"OK," said River quietly. He walked to Point One, sighed and scratched his head.

"What is it?" asked Mona.

"It's Thursday already. We'll have to move all the creatures tomorrow night if we're to empty the pond before the farmers' market!"

"The ducks will follow me anywhere," said Mona. A duck stuck its head out of the reeds, quacked noisily as though in disagreement and disappeared again. River tried not to laugh as Mona folded her arms and twisted her mouth. "Anywhere with, er … a bit of persuasion. We're goin' to need grain. Lots of it!"

"I'll fix that," said River, kneeling by the pond. "I'll get jam jars to move the tadpoles and frogs. It'll have to be done carefully and the jars will need lots of air holes. How many d'you think there are?"

"Too many," said Mona. "Tried startin' a frog choir once. They were all over the place."

River trailed his net beside the bank. When he lifted it up, it was filled to the brim with frogspawn. Angry-looking toads sat on its top and leaped over his head. "We're going to need a bigger net."

"You have to be brave
to save someone's dream,"
said a wise owl.
"Dreams have wings,
so hold on tight."

Chapter 9

Crouching in moon shadows, Dashbuckle watched Mona and a boy from behind a rock.

"Pond drainin'!" he cackled, tramping back to the swamp. "Why didnst I think of that?" he asked a beetle. "I wonders if that nincompoop Fergus's got enough buckets to empty that pond before they gets me treasure?"

"Bucket's only half-good for that job," said Fergus when Dashbuckle told him the plan. "I gots somethin' better than that."

At Fergus's shack on the edge of the village, Fergus showed Dashbuckle his antique, manual vacuum cleaner – the Stompity Pumpity. "We could drain the pond and scoop up the treasure with this," he said.

Dashbuckle inspected the odd contraption, which looked like a broom attached to a box, and wondered if Fergus was related to a sea sponge.

"We can't be *sweepin'* the water out. You, boy, are one of the El Stupidos."

Fergus didn't answer. He just tramped on two step-pumps either side of the vacuum cleaner. When the wheezy noises started, Dashbuckle jumped to the ceiling. But as he watched Fergus's machine sucking dust from the floor, an idea went up like a flag in his piratey black eyes.

Sometimes the El Stupidos see things in a different light. So stupendously stupid are they, that they see a hat in a fruit basket, a comb in a fork and a pond-drainer/treasure-catcher in a *vacuum cleaner*. Tomorrow Dashbuckle decided they must test this apparatus on another pond, where folks wouldn't see. Then by nightfall they could empty the Big Deep in one go!

At sunrise Dashbuckle followed Fergus with his Stompity Pumpity over fields to a small pond on Pigpot Farm.

"'Ello, fairies!" Fergus called out as they passed a circle of daisies. "That's a fairy ring. Bad luck not to say 'ello to the fairies."

"Ye'll be 'elloing fish at pond's bottom if ye don't shuts it," growled Dashbuckle, trying to stamp on the flowers.

Fergus screeched when butterflies appeared from nowhere, fluttering madly over his face. "You've made the fairies angry!" he yelled. "They'll be after you."

Dashbuckle gave a nasty grin and air-trampled a few more flowers.

When they reached the bank of Pigpot Pond, Dashbuckle told Fergus to "Start the sucker-upper!" Fergus stamped on the vacuum cleaner and it spluttered into action, sucking up pebbles and grass. He pointed the nozzle at the surface of the pond and, with a whoosh, it sucked up the water. "Sharkey malarkey! 'Tis workin'!" Dashbuckle cried.

An audience of sheep *baa*-ed in agreement, liking what they saw. The vacuum's bag grew rounder, gurgling as the small pond slowly shrunk.

"Bigdeepby Pond after this!" said Dashbuckle.

There came clunking sounds as pebbles from the pond bed scuttled into the bag, which was now as plump as a big balloon. Fergus yelped as the vacuum cleaner shuddered and shook.

BANG!

The bag exploded. Water burst from holes in every direction, stones pinging like bullets, and the vacuum rocketed to the sky, with Fergus still clinging to it.

"WAAAAAAAAAAH!" he screeched, shooting through the air and landing upside down on a tree.

Dashbuckle roared in anger as water, pondweed and pebbles shot through his ghostly form.

"Ow!" said Fergus, swinging from his knees on a branch. "Fink we're gonna need a bigger bag."

*"Don't bite off
more than you can chew,"
said the giant to the caterpillar
on the beanstalk to the sky.*

Chapter 10

After school, River hung his backpack in the hallway. He brushed past his mum's drainpipe harp and it jangled as he tiptoed over more of her creations, like guitars made from bicycle wheels and tambourine boots. From the living room came the sound of cats and pigs fighting. River stuck his head round the door and found his mum giving violin lessons to a girl with long hair.

"Have we got any empty jam jars?" asked River. He didn't normally interrupt his mum's lessons, but this was an emergency.

The girl turned and looked at him. It was Kaleisha. Her plaits were gone and her hair was wavy as an ocean. She smiled and gave a little wave. River grinned back, even though he was surprised to see her.

"There you are!" said River's mum over her glasses. "I wondered where you'd got to. Thought you'd gone fishing early for our tea." Her eyes twinkled as she pretended to look serious. "I wanted to ask you about that mysterious fish on the radiator this morning."

"That was Boot!" said River. "You shouldn't have put him in the washing machine."

"A boot?" said his mum, and laughed, posing with her foot in the air as though showing off a new shoe. "Well, isn't fashion fun these days?"

Kaleisha giggled and shared a look with River. Somehow, he didn't feel quite as embarrassed at his mum's antics as he did in front of others. He sighed and said he needed jars for a rescue mission. Before his mum could answer, Kaleisha told him there were boxes full of them in her shed and that they were his for the taking.

River smiled until he saw Mum beaming at them. She was always doing this: trying to get him to make friends and practically blowing a bugle if he ever spoke to anyone. She announced that the lesson was over. "Now, off you run, you two, and have lots of fun. Just don't rescue any runaway jam!" she said.

Laughing, Kaleisha packed up her violin and followed River to the hall. *OK*, thought River, *that joke was a bit funny*, and he rolled his eyes with a grin.

"I didn't know that was your mum," said Kaleisha as they left the cottage.

"Yeah," said River uneasily. He knew some people thought she was a little odd because she was so different. He really hoped Kaleisha didn't think so.

"She's so funny. I love her jokes," said Kaleisha. "She was showing me all the instruments she's made. And she's a great music teacher. You must be amazing on the violin."

"Amazing at playing bongos on it," said River.

"Shame," said Kaleisha and they both smiled.

"I actually play the ukulele," said River, as they turned onto the busy sunlit square. "We had a band with my dad when he was here."

"Oh," said Kaleisha. "I'm sorry. Is your dad" – she paused and then said quietly – "dead?"

"Sort of," said River. "He's a zombie."

"Zombie?" said Kaleisha, tripping on cobbles.

"He's in another band now," he said, grinning. "Zombified, they're called. I see him on tour breaks and stuff."

"Cool," said Kaleisha.

River felt awkward talking to most people, but not Kaleisha. It felt easy somehow, even the quiet parts. They passed the village shops and turned up the second lane towards her cottage.

"Is that a badger in your backpack?" asked Kaleisha, peering under the flap. "So cute!" She lifted her gaze to meet River's eyes. He was taken aback by how twinkly hers were, like stars in a pond, and it took him a second to answer.

"Er … yeah," he said. "I call him Boot." He twiddled his fingers, worried she was going to laugh at him for carrying a "toy" around, because to everyone except River and Mona that was all Boot was.

"Cool name for a badger," she said, opening the gate.

Boot thought Kaleisha was a cool name for a girl. He knew a lot about these things. And Kaleisha was pretty, even though she had no striped snout or wobbly underbelly. The way she played the violin could frighten foxes; what wasn't there to like? Overall, Kaleisha was super-cool. There was no more to be said.

River smiled. He thought Kaleisha was super-cool too.

"On the ice cream of life, friends are the sprinkles," said a wise ant.

Chapter 11

"THIS WILL EMPTY THE POND!" Dashbuckle pointed at a leaf-suction machine on the box of visions called "Tee Fee". His shadow in the afternoon sun looked like a sea monster across the peeling waves of wallpaper. He jumped back over a small "So faar" made of mopheads in Fergus's hut. Fergus sat eating biscuits.

Fergus nodded at the telly, spluttering crumbs. "I know a farmer with somethin' better than that. He's got a manure collector. It'd suck up the pond in no time. Better than the vacuum cleaner!"

"What be ye waitin' for?" snarled Dashbuckle. "I'LL BE HAVIN' IT NOW!"

Dashbuckle stamped across the muddy yard of Riffchaff Farm. Fergus had been looking through barns and sheds for hours. It had turned out that Fergus knew which farmer had a manure collector but had no idea where it was kept. "And I can't be askin'," he'd told Dashbuckle, "'cause of a fallin'-out over a chicken."

Muffled cries came from inside a haystack and Fergus tumbled out into the farmyard. "Shh. Landlubbin' farmer'll hear ye!" hissed Dashbuckle. "Find this dung gobbler before I turn ye into a scaredycrow." Then he spotted the biggest barn yet. The sign above the door read: *Big Tractorsaurus!* Now that looked more like it.

Whistling, Dashbuckle peered around a tall, creaking door and then stepped in. An enormous tractor with a long, stretchy pipe and massive tank stood in dusty slits of sunlight. "That's it! The Mucksy Deluxy!" said Fergus, appearing behind him.

"'Tis a ship of dreams!" said Dashbuckle, cackling as Fergus scrambled up its sides. "Better

launch this brummin' bull trout on the open road!" He leaped aboard the tractor as Fergus started the engine. "Treasure awaits!"

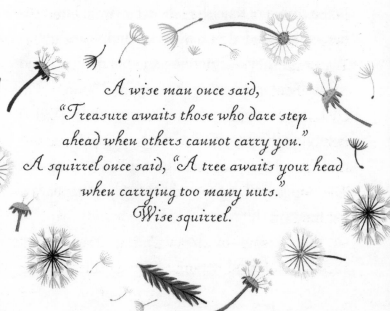

A wise man once said,
"Treasure awaits those who dare step
ahead when others cannot carry you."
A squirrel once said, "A tree awaits your head
when carrying too many nuts."
Wise squirrel.

Chapter 12

"So, what's the rescue mission for?" asked Kaleisha. River was looking at the wormery that sat in the corner of Kaleisha's shed. He turned towards her as she handed him a box of empty jars.

"Er … they're emptying the pond soon," said River. "So, I'm rescuing the frogs and stuff."

Kaleisha tapped her chin thoughtfully. "Who's emptying the pond?"

"They, er…" River pretended to look for something while he thought about how to answer. He had a feeling he could trust her, but what if she didn't believe in ghosts? "It's a secret," he said. "But it's for a good reason."

Kaleisha's eyebrow lifted, but all she said was, "Oh, OK. You'll need wheels for these jars anyway." She uncovered an antique pram in a corner of the shed and lifted a box of jars on top of it.

"Perfect," said River, his eyes lighting up. They piled several boxes and crates on until the pram springs squeaked under their weight. "Have you got a fishing net?" River asked. "To collect the frogspawn."

Kaleisha looked around then pulled down a net curtain from the shed window. She curved it into a circle on its spring rod and swung it about

in the air, dust twinkling about them like snow. "Will this do?"

"Yeah, that's brilliant!" said River, coughing at the dust.

They stepped out of the shed into the sunlight.

"So, can I help with this rescue mission?" Kaleisha asked.

River moved a spider from his shoulder to a leaf. He wondered if Mona would show up with Kaleisha around. He didn't want to scare Kaleisha. But surely Mona would be glad of extra help. And maybe he was the only one who could see her anyway...

"OK," he said. "But, remember, it's a secret."

"I'm good at keeping secrets," she said and River saw her smile up close for the first time. It was so beautiful, it actually hurt. "But you don't have to tell me if you don't want to. It'll be like ... an adventure! When do we start?"

"Sort of now," said River. "Is that OK?"

"Sort of now sounds good," she said.

Boot thought getting Kaleisha to help was a sensible idea all round. There were far too many cheeky frogs for him and River to round up in one go. What they needed was a secret weapon, and here she was… This girl had a wormery, net curtains, jam jars and wheels! Those frogs wouldn't know what had hit them! Pretty soon they'd be off on their hols to Costa del Pool-Bettina before they could say Rupert Rivert-Rivert.

Oh, yes, Boot knew all about these things.

And River was very happy too that this girl with the sparkling dark eyes was helping them.

*Magical adventures may begin
with mysterious wardrobes,
boys that fly and rabbit holes
but some start with dust sparkles,
friendship and jingling jam jars.*

Chapter 13

The jam jars clinked as River pushed the pram, piled high with boxes and a tank, over the cobblestones. Kaleisha pulled a picnic basket filled with more jars on a skateboard. River's fishing net and Kaleisha's curtain net were with Boot in the backpack. Shopkeepers were closing their shops and turned to look as they crossed the square.

"There's something I should tell you," said River. Kaleisha nodded and he wondered how to put it into words without putting a foot in it. "I'm helping someone," he went on. "A sort of person."

"A sort of person?" Kaleisha's eyes scrunched up as she smiled.

"No, I mean … you might not be able to see her."

"Why not?" Her gaze never left his face but his eyes darted away.

"She's … sort of … shy," he said.

"That's OK," said Kaleisha, tossing back her hair. "I used to be shy."

River stared at her. He couldn't believe it was that easy. She didn't think it was weird and seemed to trust him, and that felt sort of amazing. A grin burst out of him.

A bounce came to his step as they approached the pond. But there was one niggle left… What would Mona think about Kaleisha helping rescue her bones?

"Is it OK to wait here while I speak to my friend?" he asked as they reached the reeds.

"'Course," she said, smiling, and sat on a patch of grass.

River nodded and disappeared through the bulrushes.

At the pond Mona sat waiting for him, her legs in the water. She looked paler in the daylight, he thought, more as he imagined a ghost would look.

"River!" she said, rising up as he
trundled the pram to the
bank. "OOH!

What
curious things be here?"
River explained that the jars
were for tadpoles and the tank was
for the frogs. She drifted around as he
untied everything. He was used to her
floating but wondered what Kaleisha
might think.

"I've brought a friend," he said
when he'd finished. "Is that all right?"

"A friend?" asked Mona, looking about.

"Yes, she helped me with all of this."

"Bobbin' bean baskets!" she said. "Lets me see
her, then."

"So, you don't mind?" asked River, but Mona

was already hovering above the rushes facing the village square.

"Be that her, over there?" she asked. Her voice was so loud the ducks came out to look.

"Er … Mona," said River, pointing at the distance between her feet and the ground. "This might look a bit strange. She doesn't know you're a…" He shrugged. "You know."

"Oh!" said Mona, sinking down beside him and flattening her flowing skirts. "Happen she'll not see me anyways. But if she does, I promise I be best behavin'." River stuck his head beside hers as she peeked through the undergrowth. They could see Kaleisha blowing dandelions and smiling as they scattered in the breeze. Mona nudged River. "She likes dandelion clocks! I like dandelions. Always did, an' always will!"

Mona blew a kiss at a fluffy duckling

that was bouncing on a reed. "Well, brings her here, then!" she said.

River ran excitedly to the edge of the reeds and waved Kaleisha over. The plan would go much faster with her help. "We can start now!" he told her.

Kaleisha jumped up in a haze of sunlight and floating seeds, dandelion stalks scattering to the ground. Moments later she pulled the picnic basket and skateboard through the reeds and past a smiling Mona to the pond.

"What a jigglin' lot of jars!" said Mona.

Kaleisha looked in her direction then turned to check out the pond. "I think we've got enough for these," she said, crouching to look at the frogspawn.

River's eyes darted from Mona to Kaleisha. He couldn't make out if she'd noticed Mona or not. And right now, Mona was hard to miss. She was in mum mode, clasping her hands together, with a smile so large it tilted her head.

"I had curls too when I were a lass," Mona said. "Good for catching flyin' dandelion clocks. All the more wishes!"

Kaleisha pushed her hair behind her ear and dipped a net into the pond. Without a word, River and Mona decided that Kaleisha couldn't see the dead and that maybe it was for the best. River pulled a bag of grain from his backpack and started scattering it.

"That'll get the ducks a-movin'," Mona whispered. "With a little help from Boot."

River caught her looking around for Boot and pointed to him, lying flat out on a shelf under the pram.

"He had a close encounter with a dusty curtain net," River explained. "Said he was attacked by sneezes and had to evacuate the backpack."

Boot looked very sorry for himself. Duck-guiding and sign-switching were now out of the question. A tough decision, but knowing when to rest and let others take over was a sign of great leadership.

"Right! Feather-coats, follow me," Mona called. "We're a-walkin'!" And she swished on ahead with the ducks, little egrets and goldeneyes.

Kaleisha and River carefully collected the

frogspawn from the pond, scooping it up into the jam jars and then placing them in the boxes on the pram. Just as they turned their attention to the frogs, there was a loud crackle from behind the rushes towards the swamp.

"What was that?" asked Kaleisha, turning around quickly.

"Don't know," River said, his heart beating fast. He stared into the reeds, his skin prickling.

Something cracked beyond the fallen tree along the bank and Mona's words, *Dashbuckle pirate came a-creepin'*, echoed in his head. He had a shivery feeling they were being watched. "Come on," he said to Kaleisha. "Let's hurry up."

She nodded, her eyes darting nervously towards the bulrushes again. "You don't think it's the Crackenlurk?" she said in a whisper.

River shuddered. "That's just a legend," he said. "Nothing to worry about. Come on, let's get these frogs and go." Grabbing a bag from his backpack, he flung peas across the pond.

Kaleisha gasped, the noises in the rushes forgotten, as frogs came from everywhere. River swept some into his net and caught some mid-leap. "Frog Tours, this way!" Kaleisha cried, giggling, before catching and plopping them into the tank.

As Kaleisha whirled about after leaping frogs, River glanced at the bobbing rush tops, an uneasy feeling in his stomach. "We should hurry," he said, tightening the washing line around the boxes.

"But this is fun!" said Kaleisha, catching another frog.

"We ... we have to follow the plan," he said.

"This frog doesn't seem to know there's a plan," said Kaleisha, laughing as she chased a frog heading for a quick swim before their journey.

After she placed it safely in a box, River took one last look around the pond. Not a frog in sight. "OK, let's go!" he said and began to pull the heavy skateboard as fast as he could towards the village square.

Krivett! came a faint croak across the rushes. River jumped in surprise.

"Sounds like a baby frog," said Kaleisha, letting go of the pram. "We can't leave it all by itself."

"I'm not sure it is," said River, remembering the terrible cry that had come from the swamp earlier.

Krivett!

River sighed. Maybe it was only a frog. And there was no way he could tell her why he was scared. If someone told him a pirate-ghost might be hanging about, he would have fallen over laughing.

"We can't leave the little thing. Come on. We'll be in and out!" called Kaleisha, suddenly running in the croak's direction.

"Wait!" shouted River, his heart sinking as she disappeared into the reeds. If there was something out there, he couldn't leave Kaleisha to face it alone. There was only one thing to do. He set off after Kaleisha in a run.

A foul stench hit them as they came close to the swamp. Squelching through green mud, reeds

scratched their arms and faces. Dark clouds rolled above and they were dipped into a grey gloom. They suddenly found themselves behind a wall of rotting reeds that seemed impossible to pass.

Krivett! Krivett!

River and Kaleisha stared at each other, then, with a huge shove, they broke through and into a glade. The ancient part of the swamp was silent as a graveyard. Bulrushes, weathered to white, looked like statues of rats on stalks, perched and ready to pounce. River's hair stood on end at their gaping jaws of teeth. And when Kaleisha grabbed his arm, he jumped.

"There's nothing here," whispered River, gripping her hand. "Let's go."

The sweet croak sounded again.

"Look!" whispered Kaleisha, crouching down. On a jagged stone sat a small frog, its skin like green satin and its eyes large as yellow marbles.

CRUNCH!

A sound across the glade made them spin on their feet. Something moved fast through the rushes then stopped. River's blood ran cold. He scooped the frog into his net and slowly they backed away.

BWUAAAAAK! A rumbling croak shook them to the core as enormous eyes glared at them over the bulrushes, pupils slit like blades of night. Warty blobs glistened on a giant toad's head as it lifted and sank.

A noise came from behind them.

SNAP!

River whirled around. For a second, he thought

he saw something black, like a hat or a huge beak, along their path. And then it was gone. Breathless, heart pounding, River turned back to face the toad, meeting its eyes as steam blasted from its nostrils and a rattle rose from its throat.

Slowly the creature lifted a webbed foot then stamped it down.

BOOM!

Mud smacked across them and the creature's eyes glared like fireballs.

Kaleisha grabbed River's hand and together they ran, leaping over stones, back towards the pond. Thuds beat after them and River yelled as reeds whipped his face.

"GO! GO! GO!" he shrieked as Kaleisha looked back, vibrations moving in. They darted through rushes, mud tugging their trainers, roots clawing clothes.

"POND!" yelled Kaleisha, diving under arches of reeds. Water glimmered ahead. They leaped over a fallen tree and ducked behind rocks at the pond's edge. "It's coming!"

A howling wind blasted over them and cut

wild streaks through the rushes.

"BE GONE!" came a cry, followed by a series of thuds. River and Kaleisha peered over the rocks, panting as they listened to the noises fade.

"It's gone back to the swamp," said River, relieved.

"Who shouted?" asked Kaleisha. "He said, 'Be gone.' Who talks like that?"

River avoided her eyes and touched his sore cheek. "I don't know," he murmured. Had the shape he'd seen been a pirate hat? He didn't know what scared him most, a pirate spook or the monster they'd just met. But why had the pirate told the monster to be gone? *Maybe it wasn't after us,* he thought. *Maybe we just got in the way.*

"Do you think that thing was the ... Crackenlurk?" asked Kaleisha.

River shrugged. He didn't want to think about it any more.

"Whatever it is, it's not invited to the pool party." He gave a small smile, trying to lighten the mood. With shaking hands, he put the tiny frog into the tank and turned the pram. Boot was still asleep on the shelf as if nothing had happened. Glancing over their shoulders, they set off to find Mona, who had to be wondering where they'd got to. They crossed the mud with jar-clinking strides.

When they had gone, reeds rustled and swayed though there was no wind at all. Grey smudges loomed across the horizon as though a twister was on its way. Crackles and crunches came from the swamp rushes, then stopped as suddenly as they had started.

*"Trouble isn't half as big
as it thinks it is.
It just wears a tall hat
and has a long shadow,"
said a wise field mouse.*

Chapter 14

"**B**ettina's going to freak out when she finds this lot in her pool," said Kaleisha, the tank splashing as they jogged across the square. Every step away from the swamp was making them feel a little calmer.

"The ducks and geese won't let anyone mess with the pond life," said River. They made their way past the lanes and shops to a sloping drive with trees.

"We're here," he said, stopping at a tall fence and looking around for Mona. It was odd she hadn't arrived. Bettina's house was only a short walk away.

River waited while Kaleisha scrambled up

a tree to check it was all clear. You never could be too careful.

"No one's home," said Kaleisha.

"Not a soul," said Mona, appearing from nowhere to hover beside her.

"Better be quick," River said, relieved that Mona was all right but also a little disturbed to see her floating next to Kaleisha. What if Kaleisha could suddenly see her up there? She might get a fright and fall. He jumped to wave Mona down.

"Ghosts are as good at keeping promises as goats with a bucket of carrots," he muttered to himself. He went to the gap in the hedge where Bettina had once jumped out at him on his way to school. After feeling about the fence for a bit, he found what he was looking for: two loose planks. He swung them apart and crept through.

"How d'you know about that?" asked Kaleisha, climbing down from the tree.

"Bettina likes hopping out," said River from the garden, remembering all the times she'd scared him on the way to school. "Like toads do," he added, thinking of the thing in the swamp earlier.

He ran to a gate that had been built to look like it was part of the high fence and tugged at its bolt.

"Wow!" Kaleisha said, eyeing the neat borders of flower beds on the lawn of the huge white house. Every plant in rows according to its height, grass cut sharply.

"Does a queen live here?" asked Mona, floating beside her.

"Bettina Murkhart lives here," said Kaleisha.

River wondered again if she could hear Mona, or if Kaleisha was asking a question. Shrugging, because it was impossible to tell which without asking, he pulled the pram in through the gate

backwards and was followed by a gaggle of pond birds.

"Not enough dandelions for my likin'," said Mona. River spotted her drifting beside the flower beds. She was wafting her sleeves, the breeze sprinkling dandelion clocks across the grass. Ducks leaped around her, hoping for bread, and quacked bossily on finding it wasn't. Kaleisha laughed. River checked the line of her eyes but found her watching honking geese waddle around the croquet hoops.

"Welcome to your new home, clucky ducks!" Mona said, hovering by the pool edge. She launched herself backwards into the water with a huge splash. "Clean water! Why, I've not had a bath for three hundred years! Cups and saucers, does it feel good! I might just move in. Fancy a fancy place to haunt!"

A duckling jumped into the water and River glanced at Kaleisha. He thought it must look weird that the tiny duckling created such huge waves, bouncing about the pool, as Mona splashed around like a mad otter. He coughed loudly as water sploshed onto their feet. Kaleisha looked at her trainers and at Mona with … was that a smile? River was just about to ask Kaleisha if she could see Mona when she spoke.

"Let's get everything in the water," said Kaleisha.

"Everything in the water!" River cheered, glad that he could put off the awkward can-you-see-ghosts? conversation for a bit longer.

"All in!" Mona called from the pool.

Birds appeared from all corners of the garden and Mona laughed as they flapped into the water. Kaleisha untied the jars and poured in the frogspawn while River rounded up the frogs. The small waterfall bubbled as they gathered clumps of earth and greenery from the flower beds and dropped them into the pool.

"Now it's nearly a pond," said River. There was a buzz among the wildlife as they settled. "All it needs is fish!"

A small caterpillar lay
on a leaf and wondered ...
if the smallest fish can
save a pond.
And the smallest child
can save a village.
Imagine what the smallest
things in the world
could do together.

Chapter 15

"Heigh-ho she goes!" hissed Dashbuckle, striding along the bank of Bigdeepby Pond. The box of treasure would show up in no time, he thought, his eyes gleaming pink in the evening light, as a rusting bell appeared on the sinking surface.

Fergus patted the Mucksy Deluxy as water vanished up its pipe. "It's a long way down," he shouted, turning pale, as he peered over the edge of the now empty pond.

The Mucksy Deluxy sucked up the last few centimetres of water and shuddered to a halt. "'Tis more puddle than pond!" barked Dashbuckle. "Now, get in with thee. Start diggin'!"

"Promise we go halvsies?" asked Fergus.

"Pirates promise nothin'!" boomed Dashbuckle. "But halvsies I'll say." Then whispered to himself, "Half of nothin'."

With a sigh, Fergus threw in his bucket and spade and climbed down his ladder to the pond bed. He yelped as he sank knee-high in stinking mud.

"Your shovel!" called Dashbuckle, warning him as it blubbed below the surface.

Fergus dragged it out and splattered himself in sludge. "*You're* a shovel!" he muttered, plunging it back in the mulch.

"If ye breaks that treasure box," called Dashbuckle, "I'll have ye fingers for toothpicks!"

Fergus poked the spade here and there through the mud. "Gets it yourself," he mumbled. "Treasure's mine too. Bossyboots ghost."

"What say thee, fishface?" called Dashbuckle.

"Just sayin' … is that a bit o' toast?"

"Last man what called me names be now sleepin' at Neptune's feet."

Fergus dug deep and hissed, "Can't be worse than your stinky feet…" Fergus trailed off.

A small box had risen from the mud before him. "GIVES IT 'ERE!" yelled Dashbuckle.

Fergus picked up the box and wiped it on his chest.

"Brings it up careful, or you gets the full nothin'!" shouted Dashbuckle.

Fergus groaned and climbed the ladder with the box stuffed down his shirt.

"TREASSSUUURE!" cried Dashbuckle when Fergus reached the bank and put the box down. The pirate tried to grasp it, his hands swiping right through. At that moment the ground trembled. Fergus cowered as loud thuds beat towards them from the other side of the pond.

The massive, mottled toad, tall as the rush tops, burst onto the bank. Its yellow eyes glared down at them and twitched.

"Crackenlurk!" whispered Fergus. He reached for a stick but froze as the toad's head twisted towards him.

BWUUAACK! came its rumbling croak, and slime clucked as the creature lifted its enormous foot.

Fergus fell flat on his bottom in fright. He tried dragging himself up, but his trousers stuck in the mud and dropped to his ankles. Wrenching them back up, he sprinted to the rushes and screamed. "AAARGH!"

Dashbuckle drew his sword at the beast. So, this was the monster that had carried him off.

"I'll be havin' thee!" he growled, his blade shaking. A tongue swooped from the Crackenlurk's mouth and passed straight through the ghostly sword. The pirate gulped. With thunderous stomps, the toad launched himself in the air. It clearly had a taste for pirate and wanted more. Dashbuckle yelped, leaping to one side. The earth bounced as the Crackenlurk landed, and the box flew right into the toad's open jaws.

"NO!" shrieked Dashbuckle as the monster swallowed it whole.

SCHHHLUP!

Its jaws snapped, splattering slime.

"'TWAS MINE!" sobbed Dashbuckle. "MINE!"

The Crackenlurk's eyes opened and narrowed on

him. In fright, Dashbuckle dived into the rushes and ran.

A crow cackled from the church spire and a bat flapped beneath its gargoyles. The Crackenlurk watched the one with the three-cornered hat zigzag through reeds. Steam spurted from its nostrils and flies swirled about its drool before its tongue took them away. After a while, the creature scratched its back against the Mucksy Deluxy until the whole machine tipped off the bank.

SHPLOFF!

The Crackenlurk looked on as the machine sank into the mud, leaving a curve like a spluttering grin. Fish flapped in puddles as the creature sniffed the air and listened to far-off voices. Its body quivered a moment then, lurching forward, it belched up the box, small animal bones and slime.

Shaking itself, the Crackenlurk blinked its pearly lids then pounded back to the swamp, the ground quaking as it leaped and landed. Behind it, reeds rose back from their bends and breaks and the rush tops brushed a gold and indigo sky as though the beast had never been. One by one, grasshoppers began to sound and, from the marshes, a single sandpiper sang out.

"All is as it should be," it seemed to say. "All is as it should be."

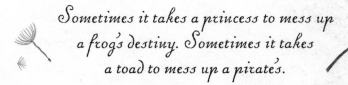

Sometimes it takes a princess to mess up a frog's destiny. Sometimes it takes a toad to mess up a pirate's.

Chapter 16

The empty jars clunked like a wonky piano as they headed back to the pond from Bettina's house. The village was often quiet at this time of the evening, so when voices drifted over to them from the pond, they stood in the square to listen.

"What is that?" Kaleisha asked.

"I don't know," River said.

The voices stopped suddenly and Kaleisha noticed that her net had fallen off the pram. "Wait for me," she said, dashing back across the square to fetch it, "and tell me if you hear any more voices!"

River wondered if Kaleisha was thinking

about what they'd seen in the swamp earlier. Then another cry came from behind the rushes. It was louder this time.

"TREASSSURRRE!"

River felt a chill creep over him.

"'Tis that good fer nothin' pirate!" said Mona, rising high in the air.

"We *did* bring him back with that spell!" River cried. A pirate *had* followed them from the swamp to the pond. He hadn't been imagining it.

"But I can't do magic!" said Mona, waving her arm. Mist swirled after it and she flapped it away. "Maybe the pebbles were magic! It wasn't me."

"You wished on a falling star, remember?" said River.

"Aye, a wisher I be, but not a magic sau—"

There came another shout. "Where be that Moanin's treasure?"

"Good fer nothin' pirate's hat!" said Mona suddenly, rising up higher and pointing. "I died-ed for that treasure! He'll not be havin' it!" She swept away, leaving a gust of wind in her path. It lifted River's hair and sent Boot sailing backwards in the pram. "DASHBUCKLE FEARLESS, STAY AWAY FROM ME TREASURE!" she roared.

"What's going on?" asked Kaleisha, running back, the net in her hand.

"Let's go and see," cried River.

Together, they ran for the pond.

Reaching the bank, they could hear Mona yelling in the reeds. "Where are you, yer kipper-stinkin' pirate?" And then they saw it.

River and Kaleisha gasped as they stared at the empty pond. A few fish flapped in puddles in a deep crater of mud and River's heart sank. "Where did the rest of the fish go?"

"Fish-napped!" Mona said, appearing from the bulrushes. "That good fer nothin' pirate were 'ere so it must be him what emptied the pond to get to me treasure!"

"Are you OK?" asked River. Mona looked so shaken and sad. Her hair was windblown and the tatters in her dress fluttered. "Why don't you sit down?"

"I be all right, me loves," said Mona, wiping a tear. "Dashbuckle's got me treasure, I just knows it! Looked high and low, I did. Could hear his piratey rat-voice in the reeds but couldn't find him. Everythin' of mine and Pa's should be back home. Bones and all!" A mouse tried putting a paw on her skirt to comfort her, but it fell right through.

"Is this your treasure?" asked Kaleisha, prodding a small box in a puddle of clear animal vomit with a stick. "It's all gloopy, next to animal bones and stuff. The pirate must have dropped it."

"You *can* hear her!" said River, at the same time that Mona said, "Me treasure." She spun around the little box and Kaleisha laughed.

"Blinkin' boot buttons," said Mona. "She can hear!"

"Why didn't you say anything?" asked River.

"Because you didn't seem to want me to see her," said Kaleisha, trying not to smile. "Thought it might bother you."

"It doesn't bother me. What about you?" he asked. "It's 'Moanie', you know." He searched Kaleisha's eyes for any sign of fear.

"Moanie?" said Mona, bouncing backwards against the rushes. "Today I was Screechy! Half-scared myself to life I did. He must have dropped me treasure that—"

"GOOD FER NOTHIN'—" shouted River.

"PIRATE!" shouted Kaleisha and they all burst out laughing.

The evening sun had spun a warm haze everywhere and River suddenly felt that everything was going to work out fine. They didn't even have to switch the signs any more to get the cows to the pond. He grinned as Mona began singing and dancing around the box of treasure. From the size of the puddle of vomit the box was sitting

in, whatever had eaten it was bigger than owls or foxes. Much bigger. River followed a trail of slime across pebbles and grass to the thicket of reeds.

"It's the swamp monster," came a whisper, and he jumped to find Kaleisha behind him, her eyes wild with worry. "Isn't it?"

River gulped and nodded. Breathless, they turned to face Mona. She looked so happy as she swung about. He couldn't tell her they had just missed meeting something as dangerous as the Crackenlurk. His lips were dry as he spoke. "It's probably not coming ba—"

QUAAAAAACK! A duck swooped low overhead, skidded past them and crashed into the undergrowth.

"Mickelmuck!" yelled Mona, running to help it.

QUAACK! quacked Mickelmuck.

"He has words!" said Mona. "Words of the doin's here." River could only stare as Mickelmuck waddled and quacked before them. "He says the one with the three-cornered hat and ladder lad emptied the pond with a hungry tractor."

River was astonished. Mickelmuck bowed at him then took a running jump at the sky and flew.

"But what about the fish?" River asked, turning to Mona.

"Fish find a way," she said. "'Tis what they do."

River felt a little better and stepped over to the bank. "At least we can look for your bones now," he said, and they stared at the drop to the pond bed. "Where should we start?"

"Could be by the bell," said Mona, pointing at it in the sludge. "But water's a rascal for movin' things. I could be 'ere, there an' everywhere."

"We'll find them," said Kaleisha. "It's OK."

They looked about for pieces of bark and slid on them like snowboards to the pond bed, then prodded the mud with sticks.

Boot stared after them and pulled a face. He did mud but he didn't do muddy mud. Perhaps someone could provide a cloak to step on. A red one would do.

Mona sighed and floated around the growing puddles. "Think I'd know where me own bones are, wouldn't you? Left 'em somewhere round here. Oh!" She stared down at something in the sludge. "Stop that ticklin'!" River squelched his way over to her. "Reckon I've found me foot," said Mona with a brave smile. He wondered how it must feel to see your own bones.

"Should we just … er … you know?" he asked.

"Dig me up to go to Dinglebeck, home to me Raphty," said Mona, her voice wavering as she sank onto a rock. "If you wouldn't mind too much."

"We don't mind," said Kaleisha, wading over to a shovel that had been left on the pond bed.

"We want to help," said River.

"We planted an oak by the inn," said Mona. "Said we'd rest there together one day."

River wanted to see Mona's face to guess what she was thinking but her head stayed low. Gurgles came from across the pond bed and he noticed that water was rising from the underground streams, but something told him he couldn't rush. He looked at the sky and the first spread of stars, sprinkled above the sunset.

"We're sort of mooncatching," he said. "Did you know we're all made from exploding stars? So, your bones are just like … star splinters."

Mona looked up, her eyes filled with tears. "'Tis the most beautiful thing I ever heard. Star splinters!" she said, looking at her stuck-out toe, her tears splashing in the mud. River plunged in his hand and gently pulled out the skeleton of her foot. "Soon be dancin' on stars with me Raphty," said Mona, wriggling her ghost feet. "Bones! Get your hat and cloak! We're goin' home!"

As darkness fell around them, River and Kaleisha helped the ghost of Mona Brightly free her skeleton from the mud of Bigdeepby Pond.

They dredged the last bone with a bucket then gathered her remains on the bank. Mona sang sea shanties as they worked on.

"*With a ho-ho-ho and a treasure chest,*
Sailor skeleton can get no rest.
Bones a-jigglin', bones galore,
Can't catch me an' me treasure no more!"

They cleaned each piece as best they could, wrapping them carefully in a bag and an old tablecloth. It felt weird at first, but River soon got used to it and Mona's cheerful singing helped. The picnic basket became the perfect place to keep the bones and treasure; safely hidden until they could find Mona's home to bury her beside her beloved Raphty.

Mona's silken voice sang across the cool night air and over the little village that had been her home for centuries.

The people of Bigdeepby, dreading wails and moans from their very own spook, were soothed with sweet and hopeful sounds and lulled into a deep and peaceful sleep.

Not all sleepers dream sweet.
But this night they did.

Chapter 17

Under an orange moon they arrived at Kaleisha's shed. The picnic basket with Mona's bones and treasure was balanced carefully on the pram. Boot was sitting on it for good measure, having made River swear that even if a tornado with flying monkeys struck, they wouldn't let go.

River searched the shadows of the trees along the fence. His heart stopped when he thought he saw cowering figures by the shed, but they were only bushes. "We'll find a good place to hide your treasure until we get you home to Raphty," he whispered, seeing Mona's eyes narrow, watching all around.

"Aye," she said. "Can't be keepin' it in me ghost cloak. Even if I could carry it, there's too many holes in the cloak. All holes, actually. Not trustworthy."

Boot agreed. He knew all about these things. Voles couldn't be trusted. Far too many of them.

"We need to find somewhere. That pirate'll be back," said River. "He wants the treasure and won't stop until he's got it."

"What about the wormery?" said Kaleisha.

"An amazing idea!" said River. "Most people wouldn't dare touch a wormery. But what about ghosts? Are they frightened of worms?"

"Worms?" said Mona, tipping her head. "No, I ain't a-feared of them. But … there's a hootin' good chance a certain grrfanuffin pirate might be. Aye! Sailors be superstitious, see! They believe all worms and snakes are related to sea serpents."

"Sea serpents!" said Kaleisha, covering her mouth to laugh. "They don't exist!"

"Aye, but they do. Magical creatures they be. And terrors of the seven seas to sailors!" Mona folded her arms, her eyes sparkling. "Happen to know a sailor of sorts who'd only sail six seas to avoid a certain sea serpent. A sea serpent whose sister he sold to a Scotsman. So terrified of sea serpents is he!" River saw Mona's shoulders jiggle as she fought back a laugh. "Happen to know his name an' all..." she whispered. "Dashbuckle Fearless!"

"A terrifying pirate scared of worms," said River, and that made them all laugh. They clutched their stomachs and stamped the ground, trying to keep it in. But when their eyes met, their laughter burst through the spring

night and echoed across the village, under a star-filled sky. It felt so good to laugh with friends, River wished it would never end.

"Now, you twos get some sleepin' done and I'll roam the night a-guardin'."

When River and Kaleisha crept home to their beds, they didn't worry about what lay ahead the next day. River lay on his pillow and grinned, knowing that only streets away Kaleisha was laughing about the hiding place and the sign they'd put there…

SEA-SERPENT BABIES.
PROPERTY OF
THEIR MOTHER.

LOCH NESS,
SCOTLAND

Chapter 18

A rat crept along the moonlit square in search of food. When he reached the old well on the corner beside the pond reeds he stopped, his ears twitching as strange sounds came from it. And as footsteps flopped on the cobbles, the rat vanished into the rushes.

"Treacherous toad tooks me treasure," growled Dashbuckle, neck-deep in water in the well. *What a stupid place to hide,* he thought, but running away from the beast meant his legs were faster than his brain. "Gets me out of 'ere now!" His voice echoed to the top where Fergus appeared, his mouth wide open in surprise, as he leaned over the stone ridge.

"Why d'you jump in there?" asked Fergus. "Should've hid with me in the graveyard. Nuffin' can 'appen to you there." He scratched his arms full of nettle rash then his head full of spiky burrs.

"Get me out!" said Dashbuckle. "Tired as a turtle I be and drained of me floaty powers." He didn't want the lad knowing that he hadn't learned the basic ghost floaty-flying thing yet.

Fergus look puzzled, wondering what could lift a ghost. Maybe if he gave Dashbuckle something sticky to grip onto... He slapped mud onto the well's bucket and tossed it in.

The rope squeaked as it unravelled, spinning the handle fast.

"ROPE!" shrieked Dashbuckle as the bucket hurtled towards him and sped through his ghostly body. Groaning, he watched the bucket bounce up beside him then glared up at a gaping Fergus. Burrs fell from Fergus's head and fizzled through him.

"Don't call people a dope," said Fergus.

"I said … ROPE!" Dashbuckle shook his head, then looking back up caught Fergus untying the rope from the hoist. He was about to scream when the entire rope thudded through him and into the water. Seething, he pushed his hat from his eyes and found Fergus grinning above him. "Fetch the Stompity Pumpity and whoosh me up!"

"It's miles away, swingin' off that tree," said Fergus.

Dashbuckle was so angry, he shot up the walls and leaped to the ground. Fergus fell backwards in shock and landed with a thud.

"Gots up yerself, then," said Fergus, smiling nervously. "Good job!"

"What jigglin' jellyfish be this?" said the pirate, ignoring Fergus and striding past the well. He secretly felt quite pleased: he'd done the floaty-flying thing without even thinking about it.

Parallel lines of mud trailed from the pond path and into the village square. Dashbuckle made a telescope with his hands. "Landlubber wheels took somethin' thatawa—"

A terrible sound filled the air.

QUAAAAAAACK!

"The beast!" blubbered Fergus, flinging himself behind Dashbuckle.

Dashbuckle shuddered but drew his sword. If ever there was a ghost-gobbler, the Crackenlurk had the face for it. He had to end the beast. "PREPARE TO—" Then he remembered how his blade had passed right through the creature. "RUN!" he cried, whizzing past Fergus.

Something shot through the reeds and bounced off Fergus's back. "RUNNIN'!" Fergus shrieked, sprinting over cobbles. "RUNNIN'!"

Moments later Mickelmuck duck flapped out of the well and shook his feathers. *QUAAAAAACK!* he called down to his echo.

A rat ran out of the rushes, picked up a bulrush top he had just thrown and scurried back to his nest.

*"The trouble with hiding
is it can get a little comfy,"
said a mole.
"The trouble with crash-landing
is the ground," said a duck.*

Chapter 19

At daybreak River woke to a tapping sound. *Saturdays are for lie-ins,* he thought, then remembered the night before. There wasn't time to sleep; they had to get Mona and her treasure back to Raphty. Swishing open his curtains he saw a bird peck the glass and Mona hovering outside. She looked worried.

"There's trouble!" she said as he flung the window open. "That no good pirate! We must warn Kaleisha."

"I'm coming down," said River. Hopping into jeans and a T-shirt, he crept past his mum's bedroom and slid down the banisters. When he

entered the kitchen, Mona sailed in through the back door. Her pale face had lost its glow and shadows circled her beautiful eyes.

"I found tracks," she said. "But 'twas too late!"

"What tracks? What's too late?"

"They followed the pram tracks from the pond," said Mona, sitting up and clutching her hair. "I thought they might follow them and I tried to get snails to smudge them away, but it was too late. They were already there! Those good-fer-nothin's are in Kaleisha's shed!"

River's head reeled. They had led the pirate straight to the treasure.

"If they finds me treasure and me bones!"

147

said Mona, circling the table. "Well, they'll not be havin' it. Over my dead body!"

"Dashbuckle's frightened of worms, remember?" said River. "He'll never find it! And your bones are safe at Kaleisha's house in the picnic basket. Anyway why would they want a picnic basket? I don't think pirates are famous for their picnics."

"S'ppose not," said Mona, wafting about anxiously.

"They'll never look there," he said, pacing to the window. "But we need to warn Kaleisha."

"Are you OK, River?" came Mum's voice from upstairs.

"Yeah, Mum," he called up. "Just getting a drink." He listened to her go back to her room then closed the kitchen door and picked up the phone on the wall. Mona swished over to see, looking curious.

"It's an invention for talking to people far away," said River. "We swapped numbers last night."

Mona looked puzzled. She jumped when he pressed the buttons and they beeped.

"It's River," he said when Kaleisha answered with a sleepy *hello*, holding the receiver so Mona could hear. Mona looked at the receiver warily like it might bite her.

"Hi," said Kaleisha through a yawn. "River, do you know what time it is?" River heard another voice from inside Kaleisha's house. "It's OK, Dad. It's for me. Yes, I've told him it's very early for a phone call," she called then spoke quietly, "Is everything OK?"

"The pirate and Fergus got into your shed!" said River. "They followed the muddy pram tracks. There's no way Dashbuckle will look for the treasure in the wormery with the sign we put up. But stay out of their way."

"Oh, no!" whispered Kaleisha.

"What is it?"

"Mona's bones! I was going to bring the basket into the house, but I forgot all about it! It's still in the shed."

River and Mona stared at each other.

"If they gets me bones," she said, "I'll never get home!"

"Are they still in the shed?" asked River.

"It's hard to tell from here," said Kaleisha. "I'm in the kitchen and you can't see that part of the garden. Wait! I've had an idea. There's an outside bolt on the shed door… If they're still inside, I can sneak up on them and lock them in until you get here! Then even if Dashbuckle walks through walls, he can't take anything with him."

"He'll not a-learned the walkie-through yet," said Mona. "Him bein' a new ghost and very stupid too. But tell Kaleisha to take great care."

"Don't worry," said Kaleisha. "I will."

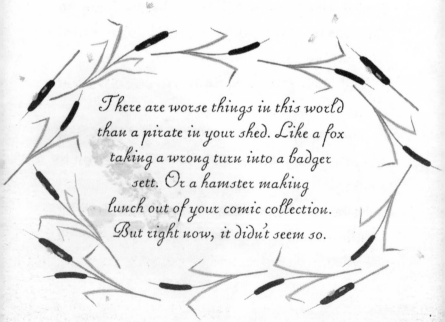

There are worse things in this world than a pirate in your shed. Like a fox taking a wrong turn into a badger sett. Or a hamster making lunch out of your comic collection. But right now, it didn't seem so.

Chapter 20

Dashbuckle and Fergus sat pressed against the shed door snoring loudly, quivering cobwebs. They'd stayed the whole night, hiding from the Crackenlurk. At first light, when the faint buzz of bees outside began, they woke with a start.

"Reckon the beast's lost our scent?" asked Fergus.

Dashbuckle held his ear to the door and scowled. "Always wait for a storm to settle afore shimmyin' up the crow's nest," he said. It was quiet outside but he wasn't taking any chances. That beast had tracked them all the way through the village. They'd been lucky to spot this shed, otherwise they would have been Crackenlurk snacks for sure. He looked about him now. It had been too dark to see much last night. Then he saw something that made his eyebrows jiggle: pram tracks on the dusty floor. "Toads throw up hard things from their bellies," Dashbuckle said. "Them pond-kids could have found... Why, the treasure could be 'ere!"

"I'll finds it!" said Fergus and set about slinging drawers and scattering screws. Dashbuckle wafted his arms as objects flew through him until he noticed a note on a cloth covering something large.

"S-S-SEA-SERPENT B-BABIES!" he yelled, leaping across the shed.

"Aw! Let's 'ave a peeps!" said Fergus, pulling off the cloth. He gasped. Plump pink worms wriggled and slithered through earth and rotting food behind glass.

"LEAVE 'EM!" screamed Dashbuckle. "CURSED THEY BE! CURSED!"

"They's all pink and cuddly!" said Fergus, unhooking the glass cover. "Nuffin' to be scaredy-cats about."

"DON'T LET THEM OUT!" shrieked Dashbuckle, landing on a barrel.

"Ain't never had no baby sea serpents in me hand before!" said a sulking Fergus, flopping onto a picnic basket. "They's so cute an' everyfink. Why's you scared of 'em?"

"'Cause I wronged their ma, didn't I? Their … sea-serpenty mother!"

Fergus stared at the worms. "Them there things' mummy?" he said. "Aw! She should be 'ere lookin' after her babies!"

"Aye!" said Dashbuckle gruffly. "She… could… be … anywhere!"

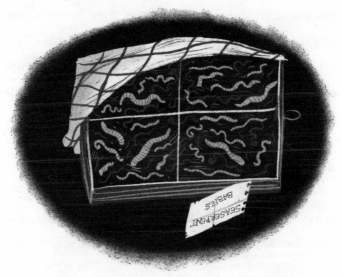

The door suddenly shuddered and rattled. Dashbuckle's legs gave way and he landed on his bum.

"Could be 'er now," said Fergus, striding to the door. "Lets 'er in, shall I? MUMMY'S HOME!"

"She's outside the door! Don't … move!" hissed Dashbuckle, and Fergus froze like a statue. "We be gettin' out of 'ere now, even if we 'ave to cuts a hole in the roof!"

"Can't you float through the walls or summat?" Fergus asked.

Dashbuckle tried twice, but he couldn't do it. "I'm not goin' out there alone!" he growled, rubbing his shoulder. "Make a hole, now!" he shouted, to stop Fergus from asking any more questions.

Fergus tried to open some shears. "They's rusty and stuck! What's so wrong with a sea-serpenty mother anyway?"

"I am savin' your life, El Stupido! Gets clippety-clippin' or you will die a terrible death by sea serpent!"

Terrified now, Fergus dunked the shears into a tub of oil to get the rust off and then scrambled onto a stool. Oil splattered down his arms and face as he thrust them through the ceiling. Fergus and the shears shrieked as he cut the roof and wrenched it back. Dashbuckle had shoved himself halfway through it when...

WHOOSH!

Cold water gushed from above.

"Sea serpent!" cried Dashbuckle, diving back in the shed as Fergus toppled to the floor. "Blast her demon tongue!" Water beat the windows like drums. "She's tryin' to drown us." He scurried to a corner and twitched. "SORRY! SORRY!" he screamed. "I NEVER SHOULD HAVE SOLD YOU TO THE SCOTSMAN!"

Chapter 21

"They tried escaping through the roof but I turned the hose on them!" said Kaleisha as River and Mona came running up the driveway. A fox on his sunrise scavenge dived through the hedge at the sound of River's feet pounding the gravel.

"The last thing I heard was, 'Sorry,' and something about a Scotsman," said Kaleisha, laughing. "Dashbuckle was so scared he thought a sea serpent had somehow slithered from the pond to my shed."

"The note worked! He thinks you're the sea serpent he sold!" said Mona, tossing back her head. "Wished I'd seen his weaselly face!"

River smiled too. He wasn't sure that the rusty old bolt on the door would keep the pirate trapped for long. He should have known that clever Kaleisha would think of a plan.

"Now we're all here, we should probably let them out," he said.

Boot rolled over in the backpack with a groan. What was that about getting out? No thank you. He didn't do mornings. His nose told him a storm was on its way but, not wanting to be a party pooper, he said nothing.

"Yeah," said Kaleisha. "We can't leave them in there for ever."

"I'll open the door," said River, his stomach leaping a little at the thought of coming face to face with Dashbuckle. "You blast them and keep doing it until they tell us whether they've got the treasure. It sounds like the sign put them off searching the wormery, but we can't be too careful." Kaleisha nodded, both hands ready on the water pressure valve. He turned to Mona, but she was holding her head and swaying. "Are you OK?" he asked.

"Feel ... a little strange, that's all," she said, lying down on the grass. "I be a bit of a weather witch. I think there's a storm a-brewin'. Happen it's that."

"Don't worry, I know how to spook them," said River kindly. "Maybe you can rest."

"Restin' ain't for ghosts!" said Mona, springing up like a plank from the ground. "I'll help!" She steadied herself and gave them a wink.

River smiled a moment then saw her eyelids, dark and heavy, and knew something was wrong. He was worried about her, but he also knew the best thing he could do right now was to check that her treasure was safe. "Let's do this!" he said.

"MMNOOO! DASSSHBUCKLE!" he called, in his best sea-serpent-sounding voice. "I'm coming to get you, SEA-SERPENT SNATCHER! You sold me to a Scotsman, now it's YOU THAT I'M AFTER!" He rattled the door and Kaleisha took aim with the garden hose. Jolting the bolt loose, River threw back the door and...

PFWOOOSH!

Kaleisha blasted water through the shed doorway with clatters and crashes as shelves tumbled and paint tins rolled out into the garden.

"Out with thee!" said Mona faintly. River worried as she wobbled but he had to keep his eye on the door. At any second Dashbuckle and Fergus would come charging out and he needed to be ready.

But no one came.

After a while, Kaleisha turned off the hose and threw it down. River and Kaleisha crept closer to the open doorway.

Behind them Mona gave a shriek. They turned to see her flying towards them as though pulled by an invisible rope from inside the shed. They ducked just in time to avoid her passing right through them.

"They've gone and got me bones!" said Mona, as she catapulted into the shed. They grabbed at her arms and dress, but their hands passed through. In a flicker of light, Mona was dragged through a hole at the back of the shed.

"MONA!" they shouted but it was too late. Mona was gone. River looked at the rotten planks and the kicked-out hole beside the puddled floor.

They'd stopped the pirate and Fergus escaping from the roof, all right, but had forced them to make a new getaway. Now the pirate and Fergus were gone, Mona's bones with them.

Kaleisha clasped her hand to her mouth. "Oh, no! It's all my fault! If only I hadn't left the picnic basket in the shed. They must have found it and taken it! I'm so sorry." Her eyes filled with tears.

River was distraught, but he didn't want Kaleisha to feel bad. "It's OK. It was an accident."

Kaleisha shook her head in misery and then climbed through the hole in the wall. River

followed her out into the sunlight. Together they stood and stared at the grass fields before them, swaying like a rolling sea. Pointer's Peak loomed in the distance, grey clouds growing above it. There was no sign of Mona. A piercing thought shot through River that he might never see her again.

"MONAAA!" he shouted.

Beside him Kaleisha began to cry.

Thunder rumbled above them and it began to rain.

"Storms may tumble around you,
but all things grow from the rain,"
said the big dandelion to the little one.

Chapter 22

A loud rumble shook the sky.

"Listen how loud me tummy's grumblin'! Lucksy I grabbed that picnic basket," said Fergus. "It's hungry work, knowing we were nearly a sea serpent's breakfast."

"That's thunder, you..." Dashbuckle couldn't waste words on this El Stupido any longer. They had stopped in a field to catch their breath and found themselves surrounded by sheep. Dashbuckle sat on a rock and stared around fearfully. The sea serpent didn't seem to be following them, although you couldn't be too careful.

Fergus opened the basket and sniffed some

jars. "Urgh, frog jam!" he said, and flung them away. He pulled out some old crackers from under a tablecloth. "AARGH!" he cried, staggering back. "Basket's a dead man's chest! It's full of bones!"

Dashbuckle edged closer to the basket. "Those bones be old as me own... I reckon they're the bones of Misha Brightly."

A plan began to form in his mind. Them landlubbers had the treasure somewhere. Sea serpent or not, he needed that treasure. He couldn't come back to life without the Lunalixir and he couldn't be rich without Mona's treasure. The answer was all laid out like a pretty picnic.

If he and Fergus had Mona's bones, maybe a swapsies was called for…

A curtain of rain was fast approaching, and… something else. He got up and peered into the distance.

Something out there was moving. A billowing shape. The something struck a tree between the fields… Dashbuckle's heart flipped – was it Mummy Sea Serpent? He stared a bit harder, his legs wobbling under him.

In a swish of light something hit him full in the chest, and Dashbuckle found himself flat on the grass, his nose propped up by Mona's finger.

"GIVE ME BACK MY BONES OR I'LL FEED THEE TO A SEA SERPENT! YE FLEA ON A SHIP'S RAT!"

Sometimes, on this small blue planet, when folk believe things could not get any worse, things get a little bit better. Usually followed by even worse.

Chapter 23

"She's such a sweet person," said Kaleisha, looking across the fields behind the shed. "And now she's alone with that horrible pirate! And it's all my fault."

"We'll find her," said River, squeezing Kaleisha's hand. "Mona wouldn't want you to be upset like this. It was a simple mistake. Don't worry. They can't have got far with her bones." He knew ghosts couldn't carry bones so Fergus must have carried or dragged the basket by himself. And that would leave tracks. They could follow them. But why would they want Mona's bones? It was the treasure the pirate was after, and that had been left in the wormery.

Kaleisha nodded sadly. "We have to find a way to get her back."

Thunder roared again and flickers of lightning followed. The hairs on River's arms stood up as the sky darkened. "Yes, and we'll think of one. Then as soon as we get her bones back, we'll take them straight to Azakeyle's Inn and bury them so there's no chance of the pirate stealing them again. We should find out how to get to the inn."

"I looked it up online last night," Kaleisha said. "She lived in Dinglebeck. I printed a map and everything." She pulled a folded piece of paper from her pocket.

River could have hugged her. "Kaleisha, you're brilliant!"

Boot thought so too. Her water hose skills, however, were on the carefree side… He and the backpack now had wet bottoms from being left on the ground in the splash area.

River picked up his dripping wet backpack with Boot drooping out. "I think we need a radiator for these," he said.

Boot agreed. A raving gator was probably the only thing to get them dry.

"And we'll need something to eat and drink," said Kaleisha. "It's a long way to Dinglebeck."

"Yes," said River. "But we need to be quick. Mona's counting on us."

Kaleisha grabbed the treasure box from the wormery and together they dashed into the kitchen, where they put Boot and the backpack on the radiator to dry while they grabbed supplies.

"Right," said River as they hurtled back into the garden. "Let's look for tracks to find that good fer nothin' pirate."

He was cut off by a rock hurtling past them

and hitting the window of the shed, showering glass everywhere.

The note fastened to the rock read:

IF YOU WANTS TO SEE
MINA BRIGHTLY AND
HER BONES AGAIN, BE
AT POINTER'S PEAK BY
SUNSET. BRING TREASURE
OR YOU WILL NEVER NOT
SEES HER NO MORE!

DASHBUCKLE FEARLESS
AND HIS ~~KRU~~ CREW.

"Oh, no!" cried Kaleisha.

"At least we know where to find them now. Come on; let's go. Poor Mona is stuck with that rotten pirate."

They set off at a run, Mona's treasure in Kaleisha's backpack.

Don't forget me! Boot reminded them, dangling off the raving gator. He fell off with a thud. There was a long silence.

Abandoned, he thought, looking at drips coming off the ceiling.

And wet.

Left all alone in a house with a washing machine.

Friendships never la—

River ran indoors and grabbed him and the backpack.

Friendships last for ever.

Chapter 24

*There are times in this life
you just want to be the back
of the pantomime horse and let
someone else lead the way.
Now was such a time.
But sometimes you've got to
step up to the front, put on the
ears and say, "Neigh!"*

River and Kaleisha ran between fields, towards Pointer's Peak. From a distance, River thought the peak looked like a wave with a huge drop at its end. But as the afternoon passed and they reached its broadest side, it looked an easier climb. River was nervous. What if the pirate had hurt Mona? He made himself move faster, Kaleisha jogging along beside him to keep up.

"We should have brought a plant pot full of worms," said Kaleisha, tugging her backpack. "A little present for Dashbuckle when we've gone."

"Sea-serpent babies!" River laughed, stepping over ferns at the foot of the peak. "But he might not let Mona go until he's checked the box for treasure."

"Yeah," said Kaleisha. "And it's cruel to worms."

Boot told River he agreed. No worms deserved to see Dashbuckle's fish-face that close up.

Halfway up the grassy peak, dotted with rocks and trees, they found a stream and quickly filled their empty bottles. River glanced back at Bigdeepby. It seemed so far away now. The rain had cleared and pale gold light glittered across the village and fields. Bigdeepby Pond, nearly full again, gleamed like a fallen fireball. His heart juddered at the sight of it. He couldn't look at it now without thinking of Mona. *Please let her be all right*, he thought.

Kaleisha was very twitchy and kept looking along the crest of Pointer's Peak, where tree shadows stretched towards them like a crooked hand. "Feels like someone's watching us."

River shuddered. He could see what she meant. There was a small dark cave where grasses swayed and wind-bent trees huddled behind boulders. Plenty of places for pirates to hide. "Come on," he said. "Let's get to the top of the hill."

Hitching up their backpacks, they tried hurrying along the slope but had to slow down as they slipped on moss. Roots like goblins' faces seemed to glare all around. An unseen bird twittered a warning, making them both jump. Suddenly a crack sounded above them.

"Look out!" called River, and they threw themselves to one side as a rock hurtled between them and crashed downhill.

"You OK?" gasped Kaleisha, her face in the grass.

"Yeah," said River, but as he got to his feet his legs shook. He looked about for any sign of where the stone had come from. His eyes shifted from the cliff edge to the trees and boulders that seemed

ready to pounce. A twig snapped behind them and they jumped. "They're here," he whispered.

A tall pirate stepped out from behind a large rock. His piercing eyes were black as his tattered coat. He sauntered towards them in knee-high boots, his sword clinking eerily from his hip.

"Here be the tiddlers wot tooks me treasure!" Dashbuckle sneered, flexing his fingers.

River's heart thumped as he looked up at the towering ghost of a pirate. He had to be brave for Mona. "It's Mona Brightly's treasure, not yours!" he said. "What have you done with her?"

"Don't ye goes a-worryin' 'bout Merry Manda!" said Dashbuckle. "She be … out of harm's reach!"

There was a rustle in the bushes behind Dashbuckle and Fergus crawled out. "Up a tree, in't she?" he said. He let out a grunt as Dashbuckle nudged him in the ribs.

"Blitherin' blackfish! Don't go tellin' 'em!"

River and Kaleisha looked at the treetops. A sad-eyed Mona hung from a rowan tree, her hands behind her back and a gag around her mouth. She was wriggling and mumbling, but whatever held her was tied fast.

"What have you done to her?" shouted River, glaring at Dashbuckle. He didn't understand how you could tie a ghost down.

"Witchblane leaves," he said. "Magic it be. Works on all creatures. To cover that 'orrible fog horn of 'ers!"

"She's a ghost not a witch!" said Kaleisha, meeting the pirate's gaze.

Dashbuckle loomed over them and chuckled. "I not be 'ere for chitter-chatterin'." River tightened his backpack straps. "Gots the treasure in there, 'ave yer?" snapped Dashbuckle, trying to snatch a strap, but his hand swished right through.

"Set Mona free first!" said River, stepping back in fear as Fergus made a grab for his backpack. River pulled away from his grasp and ran to the cliff edge.

"Careful!" Kaleisha shouted after him.

River's legs shook as he dangled the backpack over the drop. "Free Mona or I'll drop the treasure!"

"No needs for that, matey!" said Dashbuckle, flapping his arms in panic.

"NOW!" River said, holding the backpack even further out over the edge. Kaleisha covered her eyes, terrified River was going to fall.

"Brings her down from the tree!" Dashbuckle growled, his black eyes flashing.

"And bring her bones!" called River. "We know you've got them." He waggled the backpack again.

Gnashing his teeth, his eyes darting to the backpack, Dashbuckle said to Fergus, "Do as the lad says!"

River pulled the backpack away from the drop and held it to his chest.

At the treetop, Fergus flung away the witchblane leaves from Mona's arms and legs and pulled them away from her mouth, avoiding Mona's glare. As soon as she was free, she flew through him and down the trunk.

"WAA-EE-EE!" wailed Fergus in shock as he fell, bouncing off branches and thudding to the ground. Blubbering, he got to his feet as Mona sailed over to the children.

"Mona!" cried Kaleisha, running to her, but stopping at a white circle surrounding the tree trunk. She looked at River in confusion.

"It's sea salt for trappin' spooks," said Fergus.

"I'm a ghost not a slug," said Mona, floating over it. "Unlike you!" Her eyes were wild as she flew towards Dashbuckle.

Dashbuckle backed away. "Now, now, Miza!" he said, dodging her reach. "Can't help me piratey ways!" She cornered him against a tree and twisted his ears. "NYAA!" he squawked.

River saw Fergus fumble through the bag of bones, but before he could warn Mona she yelled, clutching her arm in pain.

"Gotcha elbow!" said Dashbuckle, ducking away from Mona as Fergus held up a small bone. "Now, Fergus!"

Fergus darted for the cliff edge and flung out his arm, the bag of bones clutched in his hand.

"CATCH HIM!" shouted Mona as they set off after Fergus.

"BONES! BONES! BAG O' BONES!" sang Dashbuckle. "Stay away from Fergus unless ye want him to drop ye bones. And how can ye walk when yer bones be smashed to smithereens?"

"DREDGED-UP SEA SLUDGE!" called Mona, rising up in the air.

"Drop them and the treasure will never be yours," cried River.

A scowl fell across Dashbuckle's face. "Let's say landlubbers get their bones and seafarers get what's fair. Say … TREASURE! Now, hands it over or the bones GETS IT!"

"NEVER!" shouted Mona.

Dashbuckle sneered and Fergus began to rock the bag wildly in his fist.

"We have to give him the treasure," said Kaleisha, looking up at her. "There's no other way."

Mona looked anxiously between his backpack and her bones, as she struggled to decide what was most important. "Do what must be done," she said, glaring at the pirate.

Taking a deep breath, River dropped the backpack at the pirate's feet. Dashbuckle danced a little jig. He nodded to Fergus, who flung the bag of Mona's bones into River's arms.

"A fond farewell," said Dashbuckle, tipping his hat, its peacock feather swaying.

"Nowt fond about it," said Mona as Dashbuckle and Fergus backed away to the trees. "I BE COMIN' TO TWEAK YOUR NOSE!"

"Sweet sprite of the pond." Dashbuckle pointed at Fergus's shirt pocket. "We gots yer funny bone! If ... ye don't follow us, we be leaving it in the valley below. But if we sees ye, reckon we be keeping it for a laugh or two. Watch you flip and fly between your bones for all eternity!"

Turning blue with rage, Mona's feet flew as she spun in a wide circle.

Dashbuckle danced down the slope to the shadowy trees with Fergus stumbling behind.

"You'd better keep your promise!" River called. "Leave Mona's funny bone in the valley."

Mona sank onto a rock, her head in her hands. "Cursed be the day that sea slime crossed my path!" River and Kaleisha kneeled in front of her on the grass. Her eyes gleamed with tears in the pink rays of sunlight. "Reckon I should count me blessin's like toes … I got you threes, that's one. And if me funny bone's laughin' at bottom of this 'ere hill, that's two. Then me bones can be all bundled ups to bury me besides me Raphty. That's ten toes full of happy! But I can't wriggle them there toes till I gets back me treasure, 'tis right in front of me now."

"That's true," said River, the corners of his mouth twitching. "The treasure is right in front of you now. But it's also right behind Kaleisha."

Mona lifted an eyebrow. "What tomfoolery be this?"

Kaleisha lifted her backpack and put it on the grass. River unzipped it and pulled out a small brown box.

"Me treasure," whispered Mona. "But how?"

"We never said where the treasure was," said Kaleisha. "He just believed what he saw."

Mona gasped. "D'you mean to say we gave him Boot? He always be in your backpack."

"No, we've given him *the* boot," said River. "We put an old boot inside. Not our Boot!" Taking off his sweatshirt jacket, he uncovered the sleeping badger, snuggled inside the hood. They all giggled and Boot woke with a start.

Humans! Crying one minute, laughing the next. Of course, Boot knew all about these things. But for now, he enjoyed the pats and tickles that were coming his way.

Pats and tickles were like stripes and wobbly underbellies. There could never be enough of them.

Chapter 25

The evening sun sat in the sky like a giant orange as they scrambled downhill, dragging Mona's bones in the picnic basket Dashbuckle had left behind.

At the bottom of the valley, Kaleisha found Mona's funny bone. Amazingly, Dashbuckle had kept his promise, but maybe the threat of another ear-tweaking from Mona had something to do with it. River caught Mona twitching as they placed the small bone with the rest of them. Kaleisha pulled out her skateboard and tied the basket to it with the bag of bones safe inside.

River knew Dashbuckle could open the

backpack at any second and then he'd be back for the real treasure. "We should bury your bones before he comes after us," he said, pulling out the map from his back pocket and studying it.

"Azakeyle's Inn should be somewhere in that direction," said Kaleisha, turning River's map the right way up.

"Aye, Dinglebeck be that-a-way," said Mona, pointing to a distant hill.

"No, it be … it's this way," said River, turning the map full circle. "That's a couple of hours' walk."

Kaleisha groaned and dropped onto a grassy mound. "I used to like walking," she said.

River took out the water bottles, some black-berries they'd found and flopped down beside her. And as the evening mists rolled in, they ate.

To Boot, the rising moon was full and glistened like a frosted vanilla cake surrounded by dollops of whipped cream clouds. Everything looked like food. The berries were tasty and filled a little spot. He had to keep his strength up. A long night lay ahead and earthworms weren't exactly takeaway.

SNAP!

Boot snuggled further into Kaleisha's back-pack. Snapping sounds usually had snapping things at the other end of them.

SNAP!

River glanced at the dark woods behind them. A bird took to the sky and an owl hooted. River glimpsed glimmers of light... Were they eyes or leaves? Had Dashbuckle discovered the fake treasure? He shivered. He didn't want to find out. "I think we should get moving," he said.

The others agreed and they hastily packed up their things.

Silently they set off in a run, aiming to put as much distance between them and the thing in the wood as possible.

"Looks familiar to me now," said Mona as they walked a path on its lowest rise up a hillside surrounded by farmland. Her hair was swirling silver-blue, although there was no breeze. "Can feel it in my bones. Gettin' closer to home… And to Raphty, under our oak."

"Not far on the map," said River quietly, his feet aching from hours of walking. He thought about his mum and Kaleisha's dad and how worried they would have been when he and Kaleisha weren't back for tea. But they'd come so far and couldn't turn back now. He tried to put it out of his mind. They no longer sensed something following them, but remembering the eyes near Pointer's Peak made River shiver.

Mona whisked ahead of them to a wooden post hidden in a thicket.

She read it and pointed to a misty path through marshlands. "That way!"

Butterflies fluttered in River's stomach as he looked at where Mona pointed. Something didn't seem right.

"No, I think it's more north," said River, opening the map. He looked up at the sky to find the North Star.

But Mona wasn't listening. She twirled in the air to see the landscape. "I'll go a little ways ahead. See if yonder path be passable for paws and picnic baskets. Wait carefuls now." And, following the sign, she swooped into the dark, leaving them alone.

River ran a few steps after her and called out. "Shouldn't we stick toge—" A rumbling croak echoed from the trees and River snapped off his torch, scared that the light might bring whatever had made the sound straight to them. Kaleisha grabbed his arm, and Boot shivered in the backpack.

"We've heard that croak before," hissed Kaleisha.

River stepped closer to her and looked back along their trail. They listened a while, but nothing moved in the woods.

"I think we should go after Mona," whispered River and they hurried to catch up.

Along a winding path, buckled with wheel tracks, they walked. Marshes that glugged and puttered lay either side of it. River winced at the stench and Kaleisha held her nose. Far ahead of them they could see Mona faintly through the fog. In silence, they passed an upturned elm, its knotted bark and sprawling roots like a crouched troll. River felt eyes everywhere and, looking up, found the silhouettes of birds in a tree. Suddenly his legs flew out from under him and he landed with a splat in a puddle of slime. The basket and skateboard he'd been pulling along behind him tumbled into a ditch.

"Are you OK? Let me help you up," said Kaleisha in shock.

"I'm OK!" said River, skidding on his knees and landing back in the mud. He was getting nowhere fast. He managed to grab onto the basket but the lid flipped open as he pulled himself up, sending him back to the ground with a splash.

"I *think* the slime is from the Crackenlurk!" said Kaleisha, reaching out her hand to help him. "I think it might be toad vomit." She scrunched up her nose. "It's disgusting!"

"Yuck!" cried River, flicking gloop from his clothes.

Kaleisha laughed so hard that she slipped in the toad vomit and landed on her behind, slime splattering everywhere. "Aargh!" she cried. "Gross."

River fought back the giggles and helped her to her feet. "How did the toad get this far from the swamp? Better not tell Mona that creature-eating swamp thing's about," he said, shaking off the dripping goo. "She's got enough to worry about with that—"

"Pirate," said Kaleisha. "Here's his hat." She pulled out a black shape from the puddle of gloop and held it up. Slime ran from its dangling feather and they gulped as they saw a massive bite mark on its rim. Kaleisha dropped the hat, suddenly looking scared. "Do you think the Crackenlurk got him?" she whispered.

"Could have," said River. "Can a ghost die twice?"

"Could do," said Kaleisha.

"Or..." said River, looking nervously about. "Maybe Dashbuckle left it here to make us think the Crackenlurk was here, so we'd get scared."

"Maybe!" said Kaleisha. "That makes more sense. It did seem odd that I could touch a ghost's hat, and how would the Crackenlurk be this far from home? They probably found the treasure was missing and followed us. They wanted to frighten us." She glanced about and then whispered, "They could have gone over the hill and be waiting somewhere ... along this path!"

River shivered as they looked at the dark blue horizon.

Suddenly something dropped from above and landed in front of them. They screamed as the thing straightened up. It screamed back at them in fright then pushed its billowing hair out of its face.

"S-sorry, me loves," said Mona. "Thought the path was higher up. Phew!"

"Mona!" gasped River with relief.

"Are you all right, me buttercups? You look proper collywobbled. Didn't mean to scare you."

Kaleisha and River exchanged a glance.

"We think Dashbuckle's found out we didn't give him the treasure and now he's trying to trap us. We found his hat in this pool of goo," said Kaleisha.

River picked up the dripping hat to show her.

"Can't see nothin' through it," Mona said. "'Tis more goo than ghoul. And that feather be more pigeon than peacock. This be a fake hat. So, they be tricksin' us into thinkin' Dashbuckle was Crackenlurk supper! I bet that good fer nothin' pirate got Fergus to move the sign too, to make us come down here."

"The map *did* show it was the other way," said River a little grumpily as they hurried back to the signpost. "We'd be there already if someone had trusted my map reading." He pretended not to see their smiles at his stroppiness as he marched past.

"Upside-down map reading," whispered Kaleisha.

River flushed angrily and followed glow-worms flickering along the path, striding ahead of the others, but only for a moment. He stopped and gave Kaleisha a shrug and a smile. He knew their journey was too important for sulking.

And even though he liked a sulk or two himself, Boot agreed. They hadn't come this far to slip on a sulk. Mona had to get home.

Chapter 26

"**C**rab-jiggin' curses!" growled a large rock in the marshy bog. The rock appeared to have a hat and turned out to be Dashbuckle. He stepped onto the path and stamped his boots. "Those squid kids and me treasure were only steps away from falling into the bog and being in me clutches," he complained to Fergus. "I tricksed 'em good with that toad vomit puddle we found, the sign and half-eaten hat. Why did they have to turn back at the last tiddlin' moment?"

The bog gurgled and a mud-covered shape crawled out of it onto the path. "*Blub duberry glug blub*," said Fergus, only the whites of his eyes visible.

"Speak propers, lad!" said Dashbuckle as Fergus shook himself. Mud splattered off him and a lizard landed on a branch near Dashbuckle's ear.

"Big warty lizard!" gasped Fergus.

"Calling me a LIZARD?" barked Dashbuckle. But Fergus was gawking at something behind him and pointing straight through his ghost belly, looking panicked.

"Bog hogs!" screamed Fergus and jumped up a tree.

Dashbuckle blasted Fergus with his freezing power and shouted, "NOBODY CALLS ME— AAAAAARGH!"

Galloping wild pigs thundered their way through Dashbuckle, leaving him flat as a flea on the ground. Wisps of him floated up in the air like lots of little Dashbuckles.

"Ow! Ow! Ow!" said the mini pirates in baby voices. They looked up at a frozen Fergus clinging to a branch. "Nobody calls me a hog bog!" they squeaked.

When the hogs sounded far enough away, Fergus dropped from the tree. Dashbuckle swirled and formed into his old ghostly shape. Steam blasted from his ears as he rose furiously above a cowering Fergus. "Turtleface! Why didn't you warn me about the pigs?" he roared. "When stuff passes through it stings like jellyfish!"

"I did warn yer!" said Fergus and gulped. Dashbuckle's eyes beamed icy blue as he slowly reached towards him. Fergus whined. "Best be after 'em," he whimpered, pointing a shaking arm at the path where Mona and the littluns had left. "They's got your treasure, don't forg—"

Dashbuckle's eyes blazed.

Fergus turned on his heels and ran.

When mistakes are made,
and trouble is coming,
stand your ground
and then start running.
So said every little dog
that ever lived.

Chapter 27

The woods were thick with night mist as they stumbled over rocks and roots. They hadn't seen any more signs of Dashbuckle but River was keeping an eye and ear out, just in case.

Peerweet – whee-erree! cried a lapwing, far away in the marshes.

Lapwing in mist cries, something suddenly dies! Boot whispered from Kaleisha's backpack on River's shoulders.

"Superstitious neddy!" whispered Mona. "We be deads already."

River patted the backpack to make Boot feel better, even though he wished he could hide in there himself. When they reached the wood's edge, River could make out a small hill above the moonlit mist. A craggy trail crossed the steep slope and a mossy sign pointed up it:

O'ER YONDER HILL,
BE WELCOME INTO
THE WONDROUS
AZAKEYLE'S INN

"It's just on the other side of this hill!" said River excitedly. "We'll have to carry this now." He lifted up the picnic basket holding Mona's bones. "There's no way we'll be able to push the skateboard up here."

Kaleisha took the other handle and they staggered up the slope. It was hard going but they each felt a push of courage from being so close to their journey's end.

"Nearly home, Mona!" said River, panting, his belly doing happy somersaults.

"I know this place well," she said, her smile shining as they took the last steps up the hillside. "We'll have a good view of Azakeyle's Inn from the top."

It was as though the moon had waited to welcome them. Clouds swept away and it hung above the horizon like a huge party lantern.

"I've never seen the moon so big before," gasped River, putting down the basket. A warm breeze rolled towards them and blew back their hair.

But Mona's smile fell away as she looked down the hill. Shimmering like a silver secret in the dark green folds of the valley lay a lake. Azakeyle's Inn was nowhere to be seen.

River wondered how a lake could just appear from nowhere. He opened his map and turned it frantically in all directions. "But it has to be here!" he said. "Azakeyle's Inn – the map says it is!" He handed it to Kaleisha for help. She trailed her finger across the paper and nodded.

"It should be here," she said.

"It be 'ere all right," said Mona, her voice thick with tears. "'Tis under there." She pointed to the centre of the lake and touched her heart. "There be our oak tree."

Squinting, they could just make out the tips of a branch, like a waving hand above the surface. River wanted to drop to his knees when he saw Mona's disappointed face. "The lake must be man-made," he said. "I think it's a reservoir. This must be an old map."

"Well, I'll be," said Mona. "Looks like the Sea of Serenitatis. I reckon the moon slung its sea down 'ere so it's got somethin' more beautiful to look at." She drifted about the hilltop then tossed back her hair. "Right! Anyone for a swim?" River and Kaleisha smiled but saw the sadness behind her sparkly eyes.

"You always do that," said River.

"What?" said Mona. "Swim like a mermaid? Can't do the duck thing… Bottoms up!"

"No," said River. "Make us laugh. Even when you're sad."

"It's true," said Kaleisha. "I wish I was like you."

Mona moved closer, almost touching their cheeks with hers. "Oh, me hey diddle-diddlers! If lifetimes could be jiggled up, I'd want you twos in mine. But this was all we had, and it filled me up … with an ocean of happiness!" Mona straightened again and stared at the lake.

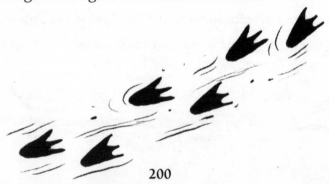

"Are you really going to swim to the bottom?" asked Kaleisha.

"Aye! The mud will bury me bones. And me Raphty's there … I'm goin' home!"

River and Kaleisha looked at each other a moment, then without a word followed Mona downhill to the shore.

A mouse crept to the spot where the friends had stood and nibbled crumbs that had fallen out of the basket. The moon twinkled in her eyes like stars. A crunch of stones sounded behind her and, with a start, she scurried away into the grass.

Now the brightness of stars
needs the darkness of night.
And even though River loved the night,
he knew nothing of darkness …
but he was about to find out.

Chapter 28

Under the dazzling moon River wondered how they were going to get Mona and her bones to her tree in the middle of the lake. She could swim but her bones couldn't. What they needed was a raft.

"What if we tied the basket onto some logs?" said River and began searching along the shore.

"There might be bits of wood over there," said Kaleisha. She pointed to a gathering of trees and ran towards them.

River swung off the backpack and kneeled on the grass. "Boot!" he said. "Stay with Mona." He rested the bag beside the basket and nodded at

Mona. She nodded back before he ran to the trees, his feet flicking up dew.

When River returned, he pulled a small boat across the grass while Kaleisha stayed behind to look for oars. They'd found it further along the shore. River was secretly relieved. He'd only seen rafts made from logs in comics. As he came closer, he could hear Mona talking. River knew the time had come for their goodbyes and stayed behind a rock to watch.

"Oh," said Mona softly. She reached over and air-patted the backpack flap. A wriggle came from inside but nothing came out. Lifting her head, she gave a curling whistle of a little ringed plover.

Boot wriggled some more and told Mona he would shortly be leaving the warm and cosy backpack but needed a few extra minutes of snooze time.

"Soon I must be leaving for the place beyond," Mona said. "To the white light we dreamed of, oceans of time ago, from our deep pond bed."

Boot was silent a moment then told Mona he needed a few minutes to tidy his fur and rehearse a speech.

Mona lifted her head to the stars and waited. Great blubbering sobs sounded from inside the backpack. River watched as the bag fell over and Boot rolled out through the flap.

"Boot," said Mona and sighed, air-stroking his fur. They looked out across the lake and swayed.

There were words to be spoken, Boot told her, but words were like worms that wriggled away from you when you needed them most. Mona told him that this was true but sometimes you didn't need words.

Sometimes there were no words.

Chapter 29

"Will this do?" asked River, smiling as he and Kaleisha dragged the small blue boat across the moonlit grass. Mona turned to look. "It's got a few holes, but a bit of bark and slime should fix that."

"How are we goin' to row it?" asked Mona.

Kaleisha leaned into the boat and held up two planks she'd found from a broken crate. The words *Juicy Tomatoes* were printed over them.

"So that's what tomatoes look like!" said Mona.

Boot had already made his mind up. Badgers and boats didn't go together, how ever much he wanted more time with Mona. Besides, he'd heard tell of flying scuba-diving otters that came at you out of nowhere from lochs and lakes.

Mona kissed his snout before they clambered into the boat. River and Kaleisha sat on either side and pulled at the oars.

They'd put the treasure box and Mona's bones in the picnic basket, and she settled beside it. Smiling, she guided them to hers and Raphty's tree.

"Such a wonderful night to go home!" said Mona, gleaming like a star creature.

"Shame I didn't bring my net," said River.

"Aye, 'tis a perfect night for mooncatchin'," said Mona, trailing her hand in the lake.

River felt queasy and he knew it wasn't from the lake. In just a few days he'd made three friends and, unusually for him, only one of them had a tail and furry ears. Not long ago he thought he'd be happy for ever to have just one friend, but now something heavy tugged at his heart.

"We'll miss you," said River, looking up from rowing. "Can you come back and visit?"

"Don't know if I can," said Mona. "But I'll

try me hardest. I'll not be missed at Bigdeepby. Happen they'll get a bit of peace there now."

River held back a sigh as they stared at the fish around the boat. Colours were shimmering on their scales like rainbows.

"'Tis magical," said Mona.

BOOM!

The boat rocked, sending the oars flying. For a second, River thought they'd struck rocks. Then a familiar voice roared out of the darkness.

"'*Tis* magical" – Dashbuckle cackled as he rushed at them – "how treasure keeps disappearin'!"

Fergus leaped out from the dark and wrenched the basket onto a small raft. Seconds later he'd kicked himself away from their boat.

"NO!" shouted River, reaching out. The boat tipped violently at the sudden movement and Kaleisha screamed as he tumbled into the water.

In a burst of splashes, River swam to Dashbuckle's raft and grabbed on, but the pirate froze him with his ghostly breath. River yelled, his hands and cheeks stinging with cold, and slid back into the lake. Water filled his mouth as he sank into the depths, bubbles like small moons surrounding him. Scrambling, he forced himself to the surface and gasped in air.

"BOY AHOY!" called Dashbuckle, freezing him again.

"LEAVE HIM!" shouted Mona.

The raft drew closer and River could see that Fergus was getting ready to swipe him. River dived below the surface. Above him was the dark shape of the raft. He swam towards it and shoved it with all his strength. It tipped, and Dashbuckle and Fergus fell into the water as River burst to the surface.

"RIVER!" called Mona, their eyes meeting across the waves. The raft rocked back up, the basket bobbing beside it. Dashbuckle and Fergus resurfaced, coughing and spluttering.

"Paddles drownded!" wheezed Fergus. He dragged himself and the basket onto the raft and paddled wildly with his hands.

Growling, Dashbuckle floated back onboard.

"GRRFNUFFIN!" cried Mona after him.

River tried to swim towards the raft, but it was moving too fast, and he was too tired.

"All yer tricksy trickery done yer no good!" called Dashbuckle. "Treasure's all mine now!"

"Hope your ears be stuck on proper," called Mona. "'Cause I be tweakin' 'em when I gets hold of thee!"

Dashbuckle cackled, but Fergus opened the basket and looked worried. "She'll be after us!" he wailed. "I don't want her hauntin' me for these skully-skellies." And lifting the bag of Mona's bones, he flung it towards her – Dashbuckle roaring as it flew.

"What dids you do that for?" shouted Dashbuckle.

River could see the bag wouldn't make it to the boat. He could hear Dashbuckle and Fergus arguing, but tuned them out. He had to get those bones. In a flash, he leaped up from the water, his arms closing around the bag – and caught them, before crashing back down beneath the water. He resurfaced with a gasp and met Kaleisha's worried eyes. She reached towards him and the boat tipped dangerously before she pulled him back in and they landed in a heap on the bottom. Catching their breath, they watched Fergus rescue their oars and the raft move away. Black ripples rolled across the water as Dashbuckle began to sing:

"With a ho ho ho and a treasure chest,
Sailor skeleton's got what's best.
Bones a-jigglin', gold galore.
Gonna be rich forevermore!"

River looked into Mona's eyes and saw no spark there. Her treasure was lost to the pirate. Treasure she had lost her life over many moons ago. A rush of blood made his cheeks burn and he plunged his hands in the water to row. "We're going to get your treasure back."

"Being with Raphty be more important than any treasure," she said. "'Tis time to go home."

"Are you sure?" said Kaleisha, her voice full of worry.

Mona nodded.

Suddenly River noticed a shape gliding through the water this way and that. They stopped paddling and stared in amazement as shining curves circled the boat.

"Whoa!" said River as the boat lifted above the surface and dropped, water splaying around it.

"What is that?" called Kaleisha above the splashes.

"She be here," Mona said calmly.

"Who's here?" said River, breathing fast. The shape ducked under the water and a moment later the boat began to move, as if being pushed by some invisible force. It went slowly at first but picked up speed. Kaleisha and River stared as they headed straight for the oak tree, cutting swerves of clear water on either side.

"What's going on?" asked River.

"I always knew she was close," said Mona.

"The Crackenlurk?" gasped River.

"Me old friend Lurky Boots? No, he left us by the shore," said Mona. "Reckon he was keepin' us safe. But that, there under, happen to be a sea serpent." River and Kaleisha stared in shock. "Just goes to show, even monsters can surprise you." Smiling, she looked down into the water. "See? The stables where Raphty an' me first met in a cloud of lantern moths."

River followed her gaze and saw a stable glimmering underwater. It was as though Mona's words had conjured the images.

"Chickens would scoot across the courtyard there, past Pa's thinkin' hut here and leave him thoughtful eggs... Blackbirds sang from the inn's roof there, when Raphty and I planted our oak, right ... HERE!" called Mona as they reached the tree.

The enormous shape swooped beneath the water, the boat spinning in its stream. Mona sat close to them until the boat settled and the

shadow under the lake had gone. "Thank you," Mona called out. "Surprises all over the place!"

Kaleisha looked nervous. "Surprises aren't as fun as they used to be," she said, and Mona tried ruffling her hair, laughing.

As a breeze scudded across the lake, River reached for the tree's leaves. Somehow, they were still green despite being surrounded by so much water.

"The tree's still alive!" he gasped.

"Aye," said Mona. "All lives on. Stars and stardust. 'Tis the way of things."

Breathing out, River knew what must be done. He lifted the bag of Mona's bones onto his lap, his hands trembling. He caught Mona watching him, her face calm as the boat drifted in slow circles.

"Goodbye, me loves!" she said, air-kissing their heads. "I wouldn't be here without you."

"Bye," whispered Kaleisha, fighting the tears.

Mona floated down into the silver water, her dress spreading like a lily pad as she stayed beside the boat.

River clutched the bundle of bones and looked into the watery eyes of Mona Brightly. "Goodbye," he said, a tear rolling down his face.

"Remember the night we were mooncatching and saw a falling star?" asked Mona.

"You made a wish," said River. "And I … couldn't think of one."

"Well, remember that wishes are like fishes. You can always throw them back till you need them." Mona winked at him and when his face didn't change, she splashed him with her fingers. River laughed and splashed her back.

"I'll remember," he said.

"I saw another falling star later that night," said Mona. "And I wished that you'd meet someone who loves dandelions like me, and become great friends."

He looked at Kaleisha and she smiled.

"I see now I don't have to hold onto the treasure for ever," said Mona. "'Tis the love that binds us, and that's the true treasure." She sighed contentedly. "The time has come … Raphty be a-waitin'!"

River watched her swirl in the water as she took one last look at the world and the moon above. Finally she nodded, and he lifted her bones and let them go. In a cascade of bubbles, they sank down through her ghostly body and deep into the water.

"Now, laugh every day," Mona said, smiling. "Always look for the hidden… And stay away from GOOD FER NOTHIN' PIRATES!"

River and Kaleisha laughed as her words echoed across the lake. Then, blowing a kiss, Mona pushed away from the boat. And as a falling star sailed above, Mona followed her bones into the depths of the lake.

Something glimmered in the water, soft and low, and orbs of colour spiralled through the darkened depths. Light swelled out from the lake with the tree at its centre, bright as day. They could see Mona diving down along the trunk, sleek as a mermaid, the bundle of bones sinking ahead of her to the lake bed. Azakeyle's Inn appeared from waves of darkness and Raphty by its door. Through a rise of bubbles, they reached for each other's hands and Mona floated down beside him.

River held his breath.

Surrounded by a swirling shoal of glittering fish and under the light of the moon, Mona and Raphty Brightly held each other tight.

She was home.

Light splintered back into the oak, shot along its branches and out to the sky like fireworks. Darkness filled the depths of the lake once more, leaving only the moon's reflection dancing on its surface.

The little blue boat bobbed and rocked, its rudder squeaking mournfully. River looked up at the enormous moon and, smiling, made a wish.

And even though he didn't tell, Boot knew River's wish was for Mona Brightly to come and visit whenever she could.

Chapter 30

"What's that hissin' sound?" said Dashbuckle.

"'Tain't me," said Fergus as they bobbed towards the shore on the moonlit raft.

Dashbuckle noticed strange ripples across the lake but hadn't the time to bother with it. He had treasure to open.

"Fortune's a-comin'!" he cried and ordered Fergus to open the box. But as Fergus lifted the lid, their faces fell. "WHAT THE SQUIDS BE THIS?" Dashbuckle shouted in dismay. Instead of treasure, there were pressed dandelions and sketches of Mona and her husband.

"The good stuff must be underneath," Fergus

said uncertainly, as he slung the sketches and tugged out several rolls of paper.

Fergus opened one against the wind for Dashbuckle to read: "*I love thee, Mona … by RAPHTY BRIGHTLY!*" With a yell of frustration, Dashbuckle ordered Fergus to rip the velvet from the box's sides. There was nothing there.

"Where be the treasure … THE LUNALIXIR?" he yelled as a corkless bottle tumbled out from the box. "EMPTY!" cried Dashbuckle. "Noooooooo!" Without looking inside it, Fergus threw it at the lake in anger. Clenching his teeth, Dashbuckle shook his fists. "BLAST YOU, MISA BRIGHTLY!"

The current was getting stronger now, making the raft rock violently.

"It's an underwater whirly-wind!" said Fergus, clinging on, as the raft rotated in faster and faster spirals. "We'll get sucked under and die!"

"SHUT UP!" yelled Dashbuckle.

"Somethin's coming," said Fergus, peering into the black water around them.

Dashbuckle peered over the water at the little boat in the distance. What was that Mina up to?

He growled as the raft jerked again. He was so angry he wanted to fling Fergus from the raft. It was then he saw an arrow of foam speeding across the lake, splitting the moon's reflection in two. Fear gripped him. Pointing at the two planks, he yelled at Fergus to plunge them into the water. "Start rowin', NOW!" he shouted.

Fergus paddled furiously but each time he lifted the oars they were drawn back by an undertow.

"FASTER!" called Dashbuckle. The thing in the water was so close he could see bubbles. Fergus screeched as a wave smacked their backs and hurled them into the water.

Dashbuckle dropped through the depths, bubbles roaring in his ears and through his ghost body like a thousand jellyfish. And when he felt about to burst, he rocketed above the surface.

"WAAAAH!" he yelled, blinking through the gloom. Two giant eyes blinked back at him and froze his ghostly heart. A sea serpent, scaly and green, rose from the water.

Fergus resurfaced beside Dashbuckle with a splash. Looking up at the fierce eyes of the serpent, he screamed.

"I ain't doin' nuffin for you no more," Fergus spluttered at Dashbuckle. "Treasure or not, I'm getting out of 'ere."

But it was too late. The pair were encircled by the serpent's enormous body and there was no escape. Shaking with fear, they bobbed in its massive shadow. Dashbuckle reached for his sword but found it gone. Ripping the braces from his trousers, Fergus took aim and threw.

"Oh, heck!" squeaked Fergus as they catapulted through the air.

SQUELCH!

They met the sea serpent's eye and fell in a spurt of slime.

MMMNNNOOOOO! it roared, swerving its neck and opening up a circle of space. The lake shook and Fergus flung

221

himself underwater, swimming for the gap and the shore beyond. The sea serpent let him go, her eyes on Dashbuckle.

"I only wished for fortune," wheezed Dashbuckle, as gaping jaws came towards him. "NYAAAAAAAAAAAAAAAAAAARRGH!"

*A dung beetle once said,
"Be careful what you wish for,"
to his friend under the cow pat.*

Chapter 31

Screams shook the night air as Kaleisha and River dragged the boat on land.

River pulled binoculars from the backpack and scanned the lake. "Look," he said. "Isn't that Dashbuckle on a teapot?" He handed the binoculars to Kaleisha.

Kaleisha giggled. "It must have been left in the basket from an old picnic."

River took another look and saw a flying fish slap the pirate's face, making him wobble. He could see Fergus now too, floating near by on top of the picnic basket and paddling frantically. Their cries echoed across the lake.

River and Kaleisha laughed and then crunched across pebbles to the bank and fell to the ground.

"Teapot!" she said, and they laughed again, rolling in the grass and stamping their feet.

"I wish Mona could see it," said River, picking up the backpack to check on Boot.

"Yeah," said Kaleisha, sighing.

Boot nestled into River's hand and sighed too.

Above them, stars clustered in the purples and blues of the Orion Nebula. They smiled, both thinking it looked like Mona, her cloak flying, towards their little village. Without speaking, they packed the binoculars and Boot snuggled into the backpack, his head poking out and resting on River's shoulder.

Turning to go, River took one last look at the lake with its moon and stars.

"Wait," he said as a sparkle caught his eye. He ran to the shore and, using his net, fished a round blue bottle from the foam. An old label dangled from its neck with a list of fruits on one side. River gasped on turning it and whispered the word written there, *Lunalixir.*

The bottle was empty, but Mona must have kept it in memory of her pa and the health drink that he had invented. And now River had something real to remember Mona by. Holding it up to the moonlight, River could make out a roll of paper inside. He picked up a stick, twisted it out and unfolded the dripping wet paper. Cut-out hearts, a cat and a fiddle, and a cow appeared, jumping over a paper lace moon. River could almost hear Mona saying the "Hey, diddle, diddle," rhyme, like the time they first met. He remembered how her pa had sung it to her every night at bedtime.

"Catch anything?" asked Kaleisha, coming towards him over stones.

A grin burst across his face. "I caught the moon."

"River," said Kaleisha, holding the paper circle up to the dark sky. "You really did!"

Of course he did, Boot agreed. He never doubted it for a minute!

After all, Boot knew all about these things.

*Not all stories end
in a happy burial, a pirate
floating on a teapot and a boy
catching the moon.
But this one does.*

Chapter 32

But wait ...
an ending here ...
when there's a swimming pool
full of pond life to sort out?
You try telling that to a duck.

"GET THEM AWAY!" echoed the cries as River and Kaleisha came closer to Bettina's house the next day. Honking geese flew above the cottages, swerving the church bells that clanged midday. The pool party was about to start, and River had a feeling it would go with a splash.

"Think we'd better get the pond life back from their little holiday," said River, running up Bettina's sloping drive.

"Yeah," said Kaleisha as the screams and squawks continued. "I can hear the fun from here!"

At Bettina's fence they climbed the tree and peered over. Bettina was yelling and shooing ducks away from illuminated sprinklers. Slipping on duck poo, she landed on her back, the sprinklers pouring down on her. River and Kaleisha laughed from the branches to see Bettina scrambling in mud, her clothes and hair soaking. River suddenly felt a bit bad, though, and hoped Bettina hadn't hurt herself.

Kaleisha pointed to the patio doors. Guests were arriving and stared open-mouthed at the animals running around the garden.

"Excellent entertainment, Bettina," said Casey, laughing as Bettina ran from charging geese. "You're hilarious!"

"THIS ISN'T MEANT TO BE FUNNY!" screeched Bettina. She looked so desperate that

River knew it was time to sort things out. He climbed down from the tree, slipped through the gap in the fence, and ran to the pool, with Kaleisha right behind him.

"Home, ducks, home!" called River. The party crowd stopped laughing in amazement as ducks flapped and waddled.

"LITTLE RIVER!" roared Bettina. "YOU DID THIS?"

Knowing Kaleisha was right behind him, confidence filled River from the top of his head to the tips of his toes. "Little River isn't my name," he said. "And maybe next time you'll think twice

about being mean to me. Or just maybe I'll bring my other animal friends to your house."

Bettina opened her mouth but closed it again as several voles skipped across her toes. "WAAH!" she screamed. "GET THEM OFF ME! Please," she said. "I hate furry things with legs!"

"We'll help you," Kaleisha said, stepping beside River, "but only if you promise never to pick on River or anyone else again."

"I promise," wailed Bettina.

"Pond life, home!" River called out and snapped his fingers. Leaping frogs, ducks and voles followed him as he opened the gate. "Tadpoles, we'll be back for you later!"

Quacks, krivetts, squeaks and *clucks* bounced across the cobbles as River and Kaleisha led the way to the pond. The bulrushes whispered welcome as the pond life hopped and fluttered into the clearing. At the water's edge River and Kaleisha talked about Mona and smiled, thinking of her and Raphty together at last.

"Bigdeepby's a weird place, isn't it?" said Kaleisha, looking across the pond.

"Yeah," said River, smiling as he sat beside a sleeping Boot. "Anything can happen."

Acknowledgements

I'd like to thank the Walker team, especially the editors Annalie Grainger and Megan Middleton, designer Chloe Tartinville and typesetter Rebecca J Hall. And of course Lia for the gorgeous illustrations.

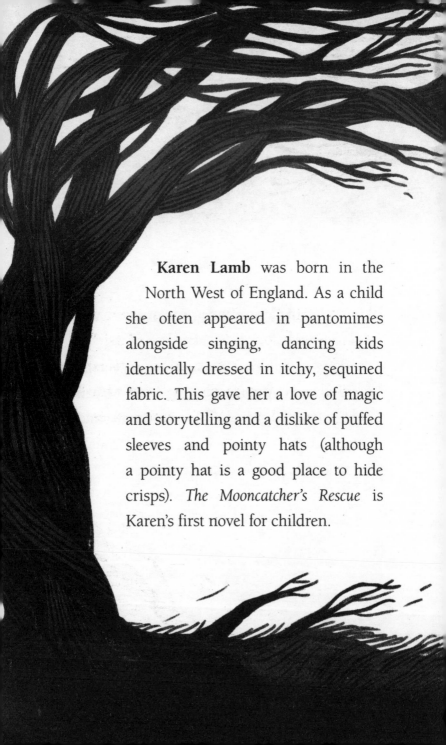

Karen Lamb was born in the North West of England. As a child she often appeared in pantomimes alongside singing, dancing kids identically dressed in itchy, sequined fabric. This gave her a love of magic and storytelling and a dislike of puffed sleeves and pointy hats (although a pointy hat is a good place to hide crisps). *The Mooncatcher's Rescue* is Karen's first novel for children.

Lia Visirin was born in a town in Transylvania, Romania. She discovered her passion for children's illustrations very early on. Today Lia gets inspiration from nature, old photographs and childhood memories.

A fantastical, botanical adventure about friendship, bravery, and finding home in a new place.

When Fern has to move to London, she feels entirely uprooted – until she meets a little plant that can understand her every word. Strange things start happening in the city, and now her new friend is starting to wilt... Can they solve this growing mystery together, before it's too late?

Sometimes you are a whisper away from magic without even realizing it.

Nine is an orphan pickpocket determined to escape her old life. After stealing a house-shaped ornament from a mysterious woman's purse, she meets a host of magical and brilliantly funny characters who have been placed under an extraordinary spell that only Nine can break…